ALONE ON A PLANET OF ALIEN MONSTERS

He awoke at dawn, slowly, dazedly, sorting out sounds, smells, thoughts. There had been a room, fear, and a man handing him a cup—that action had been very important to him, but he couldn't seem to remember any more of the dream. Then there was reality—he had been marooned on this wilderness world since he was a boy. That world was around him now, he could feel its winds, hear its sounds, taste, smell. The world of rooms and men was the dream. It had to be!

A sharp hot pain made him lose his train of thought. He looked down; from under the rocks around his feet gathered an army of blue-black, hard-shelled things, their clawed forelimbs extended, blue sense organs raised on fleshy stalks all turned towards him.

Already a black tongue of them were across his feet . . .

—from STAR HUNTER

ANDRE NORTON, one of Ace Books' most respected and prolific authors—with over forty books and millions of copies in print—is world renowned for her uncanny ability to create tightly plotted action stories based on her extensive readings in travel, archeology, anthropology, natural history, folklore and psycho-esper research. With classic understatement, belied by the enthusiastic critical reception of all her books, she has described herself as ". . . rather a very staid teller of old fashioned stories. . ."

Miss Norton began her literary career as an editor for her high school paper and quickly progressed to writing, publishing her first book before the age of twenty-one. After graduating from Western University, and working for the Library of Congress for a number of years, she began her writing career in earnest, consistently producing science fiction novels of the highest quality.

Miss Norton presently resides in Florida under the careful management of her feline associates.

ANDRE NORTON

STAR HUNTER

&

VOODOO PLANET

ace books
A Division of Charter Communications Inc.
1120 Avenue of the Americas
New York, N.Y. 10036

STAR HUNTER

I

NAHUATL's larger moon pursued the smaller, greenish globe of its companion across a cloudless sky in which the stars made a speckled pattern like the scales of a huge serpent coiled around a black bowl. Ras Hume paused at the border of scented spike-flowers on the top terrace of the Pleasure House to wonder why he thought of serpents. He understood. Mankind's age-old hatred, brought from his native planet to the distant stars, was evil symbolized by a coil in a twisted, belly-path across the ground. And on Nahuatl, as well as a dozen other worlds, Wass was the serpent.

A night wind was rising, stirring the exotic, half-dozen other worlds' foliage planted cunningly on the terrace to simulate the mystery of an off-world jungle.

"Hume?" The inquiry seemed to come out of thin air over his head.

"Hume," he repeated his own name calmly.

A shaft of light brilliant enough to dazzle the eyes struck through the massed vegetation, revealing a path. Hume lingered for a moment, offering a counterstroke of indifference in what he had always known would be a test of wits.

Wass was Veep of a shadowy empire, but that was apart from the world in which Ras Hume moved.

He strode deliberately down the corridor illuminated between leaf and blossom walls. A grotesque lump of crystal leered at him from the heart of a tharsala lilly bed. The intricate carving of a devilish nonhuman set of features was a work of alien art. Tendrils of smoke curled from the thing's flat nostrils, and Hume sniffed the scent of a narcotic he recognized. He smiled. Such measures might soften up the usual civ Wass interviewed here. But a star pilot turned outhunter was immunized against such mind clouding.

There was a door, the lintel and posts of which had more carving, but this time Terran, Hume thought—old, very old. Perhaps rumor was right, Milfors Wass might be truly native Terran and not second, third, nor fourth generation star stock as most of those who reached Nahuatl were.

The room beyond that elaborately carved entrance was, in contrast, severe. Rust walls were bare of any pattern save an oval disk of cloudy golden shimmer behind the chair at the long table of solid ruby rock from Nahuatl's poisonous sister planet of Xipe. Without a pause he walked to the chair and seated himself without invitation to wait in the empty room.

That clouded oval might be a com device. Hume refused to look at it after his first glance. This interview was to be person to person. If Wass did not appear within a reasonable length of time he would leave.

And Hume hoped to any unseen watcher he presented the appearance of a man not impressed by stage settings. After all he was now in the seller's space boots, and it was a seller's market.

Ras Hume rested his right hand on the table. Against the polished glow of the stone, the substance of it was flesh—tanned brown—a perfect match for his left. And the subtle difference between true flesh and false was no hindrance in the use of those fingers or their strength. Save that it had pushed him out of command of a cargo-cum-liner and hurled him down from the pinnacle of a star pilot. There were bitter brackets about his mouth, set there by that hand as deeply as if carved with a knife.

It had been four years—planet time—since he had lifted the Rigal Rover from the launch pad on Sargon Two. He had suspected it might be a tricky voyage with young Tors Wazalitz, who was a third owner of the Kogan-Bors-Wazalitz line, and a Gratz chewer. But one did not argue with the owners, except when the safety of the ship was concerned. The Rigal Rover had made a crash landing at Alexbut, and a badly injured pilot had brought her in by will, hope and a faith he speedily lost.

He received a plasta-hand, the best the medical center could supply and a pension for life, forced by the public acclaim for a man who had saved ships and lives. Then— the sack because a crazed Tors Wazalitz was dead. They dared not try to stick Hume with a murder charge; the voyage record tapes had been shot straight through to the Patrol Council, and the evidence on those could be neither faked nor tampered with. They could not give him a quick punishment, but they could try to arrange a slow death. The word had gone out that Hume was off pilot boards. They had tried to keep him out of space.

And they might have done it, too, had he been the usual type of pilot, knowing only his trade. But some odd streak of restlessness had always led him to apply for the rim runs, the very first flights to newly opened worlds. Outside of the survey men, there were few qualified pilots of his seniority who possessed such a wide and varied knowledge of the galactic frontiers.

So when he learned that the ships' boards were irrevocably closed to him, Hume had signed up with the Out-Hunters' Guild. There was a vast difference between lifting a liner from a launching pad and guiding civ hunters to worlds surveyed and staked out for their trips into the wild. Hume relished the exploration part—he disliked the leading-by-the-hand of nine-tenths of the Guild's clients.

But if he had not been in the Guild service he would never have made that find on Jumala. That lucky, lucky find! Hume's plasta-flesh fingers curved, their nails drew across the red surface of the table. And where was Wass? He was about to rise and go when the golden oval on the wall smoked, its substance thinning to a mist as a man stepped through to the floor.

The newcomer was small compared to the former pilot, but he had breadth of shoulder which made the upper part of his torso overbalance his thin hips and legs. He was dressed

7

most conservatively except for a jeweled plaque resting on the tightly stretched gray silk of his upper tunic at heart level. Unlike Hume he wore no visible arms belt, but the other did not doubt that there were a number of devices concealed in that room to counter the efforts of any assassin.

The man from the mirror spoke with a flat, toneless voice. His black hair had been shaven well above his ears, the locks left on top of his skull trained into a kind of bird's crest. As Hume, his visible areas of flesh were deeply browned, but by nature rather than exposure to space, the pilot guessed. His features were harsh, with a prominent nose, a back-slanting forehead, eyes dark, long and large, with heavy lids.

"Now—" He spread both his hands, palm down and flat on the table, a gesture Hume found himself for some unknown reason copying. "You have a proposition?"

But the pilot was not to be hurried, any more than he was to be influenced by Wass' stage-settings.

"I have an idea," he corrected.

"There are many ideas." Wass leaned back in his chair, but he did not remove his hands from the table. "Perhaps one in a thousand is the kernel of something useful. For the rest, there is no need to trouble a man."

"Agreed," Hume returned evenly. "But that one idea in a thousand can also pay off in odds of a million to one, when and if a man has it."

"And you have such a one?"

"I have such a one." It was Hume's role now to impress the other by his unshakable confidence. He had studied all the possibilities. Wass was the right man, perhaps the only partner he could find. But Wass must not know that.

"On Jumala?" Wass returned.

If that stare and statement was intended to rattle Hume it was a wasted shot. To discover that he had just returned from that frontier planet required no ingenuity on the Veep's part.

"Perhaps."

"Come, Out-Hunter Hume. We are both busy men, this is no time to play tricks with words and hints. Either you have made a find worth the attention of my organization or you have not. Let me be the judge."

This was it—the corner of no return. But Wass had his own code. The Veep had established his tight control of his lawless organization by set rules, and one of them was, don't be greedy. Wass was never greedy, which is why the patrol had never been able to pull him down, and those who dealt with him did not talk. If you had a good thing, and Wass accepted temporary partnership, he kept his side of the bargain rigidly. You did the same—or regretted your stupidity.

"A claimant to the Kogan estate—that good enough for you?"

Wass showed no surprise. "And how would such a claimant be profitable to us?"

Hume appreciated that "us"; he had an in now. "If you supply the claimant, surely you can claim a reward, in more ways than one."

"True. But one does not produce a claimant out of a Krusha dream. The investigation for any such claim now would be made by a verity lab and no imposture will pass those tests. While a real claimant would not need your help or mine."

"Depends upon the claimant."

"One you discovered on Jumala?"

"No." Hume shook his head slowly. "I found something else on Jumala—an L-B from Largo Drift intact and in good shape. From the evidence now in existence it could have landed there with survivors aboard."

"And the evidence of such survivors living on—that exists also?"

Hume shrugged, his plasta-flesh fingers flexed slightly. "It has been six planet years, there is a forest where the L-B rests. No, no evidence at present."

"The Largo Drift," Wass repeated slowly, "carrying, among others, Gentlefem Tharlee Kogan Brodie."

"And her son Rynch Brodie, who was at the time of the Largo Drift's disappearance a boy of fourteen."

"You have indeed made a find." Wass gave that simple statement enough emphasis to assure Hume he had won. His one-in-a-thousand idea had been absorbed, was now being examined, amplified, broken down into details he could never have hoped to manage for himself, by the most cunning criminal brain in at least five solar systems.

"Is there any hope of survivors?" Wass attacked the problem straight on.

"No evidence even of there being any passengers when the L-B planeted. Those are automatic and released a certain number of seconds after an accident alarm. For what it's worth the hatch of this one was open. It could have brought in survivors. But I was on Jumala for three months with a full Guild crew and we found no sign of any castaways."

"So you propose—?"

"On the basis of my report Jumala has been put up for a safari choice. The L-B could well be innocently discovered by a client. Every one knows the story with the case dragging through the Ten Sector-Terran Courts now. Gentlefem Brodie and her son might not have been news ten years ago. Now, with a third of the Kogan-Bors-Wazalitz control going to them, any find linked with the Largo Drift would gain full galactic coverage."

"You have a choice of survivor? The Gentlefem?"

Hume shook his head. "The boy. He was bright, according to the stories since, and he would have the survival manual from the ship to study. He could have grown up in the wilds of an unopened planet. To use a woman is too tricky."

"You are entirely right. But we shall require an extremely clever imposter."

"I think not." Hume's cool glance met Wass'. "We only need a youth of the proper general physical description and the use of a conditioner."

Wass' expression did not change, there was no sign that Hume's hint had struck home. But when he replied there was a slight change in the monotone of his voice.

"You seem to know a great deal."

"I am a man who listens," Hume replied, "and I do not always discount rumor as mere fantasy."

"That is true. As one of the guild you would be interested in the root of fact beneath the plant of fiction," Wass acknowledged. "You appear to have done some planning on your own."

"I have waited and watched for just such an opportunity as this," Hume answered.

"Ah, yes. The Kogan-Bors-Wazalitz combine incurred your displeasure. I see you are also a man who does not forget easily. And that, too, I understand. It is a foible of my own,

Out-Hunter. I neither forget nor forgive my enemies, though I may seem to do so and time separates them from their past deeds for a space."

Hume accepted that warning—both must keep any bargain. Wass was silent for a moment, as if to leave time for the thought to root itself, then he spoke again.

"A youth with the proper physical qualifications. Have you any such in mind?"

"I think so." Hume was short.

"He will need certain memories; those take time to tape."

"Those dealing with Jumala, I can supply."

"Yes. You will have to provide a tape beginning with his arrival on that world. For such family material as is necessary I shall have ready. An interesting project, even apart from its value to us. This is one to intrigue experts."

Expert psycho-techs—Wass had them. Men who had slipped over the border of the law, had entered Wass' organization and prospered there. There were some techs crooked enough to enjoy such a project for its own sake, indulging in forbidden experimentation. For a moment, but only for a moment, something in Hume jibbed at the intent of carrying through his plan. Then he shrugged that tinge aside.

"How soon do you wish to move?"

"How long will preparation take?" Hume asked in return, for the second time battling a taste of concern.

"Three months, maybe four. There's research to be done and tapes to be made."

"It will be six months probably before the Guild sets up a safari for Jumala."

Wass smiled. "That need not worry us. When the time comes for a safari, there shall also be clients, impeccable clients, asking for it to be planned."

There would be, too, Hume knew. Wass' influence reached into places where the Veep himself was totally unknown. Yes, he could count on an excellent, well above suspicion, set of clients to discover Rynch Brodie when the time came.

"I can deliver the boy tonight, or early tomorrow morning. Where?"

"You are sure of your selection?"

"He fulfills the requirements, the right age, general appearance. A boy who will not be missed, who has no kin, no ties, and who will drop out of sight without any questions to be asked."

"Very well. Get him at once. Deliver him here."

Wass swept one hand across the table surface. On the red of the stone there glowed for seconds an address. Hume noted it, nodded. It was one in the center of the port town, one which could be visited at an odd hour without exciting any curiosity. He rose.

"He will be there."

"Tomorrow, at your convenience," Wass added, "you will come to this place." Again the palm moved and a second address showed on the table.

"There you will begin your tape for our use. It may take several sessions."

"I'm ready. I still have the long report to make to the Guild, so the material is still available on my note tapes."

"Excellent. Out-Hunter Hume, I salute a new colleague." At last Wass' right hand came up from the table. "May we both have luck equal to our industry."

"Luck to equal our desires," Hume corrected him.

"A very telling phrase, Out-Hunter. Luck to equal our desires. Yes, let us both deserve that."

2

THE STARFALL was a long way down scale from the pleasure houses of the upper town. Here strange vices were also merchandise, but not such exotics as Wass provided. This was strictly for crewmen of the star freighters who could be speedily and expertly separated from a voyage's pay in an evening. The tantalizing scents of Wass' terraces were reduced here to simply smells, the majority of which were not fragrant.

There had already been two fatal duels that evening. A tubeman from a rim ship had challenged a space miner to settle a difference with those vicious whips made from the tail casings of Flangoid flying lizards, an encounter which left both men in ribbons, one dead, one dying. And a scarred, ex-space marine had blaster-flamed one of the Star-and-Comet dealers into charred human ash.

The young man who had been ordered to help clear away the second loser retired to the stinking alley outside to lose the meal which was part of his meager day's pay. Now he crawled back inside, his face greenish, one hand pressed to his middle section.

He was thin, the fine bones of his face tight under the pallid skin, his ribs showing even through the sleazy fabric of the threadbare tunic with its house seal. When he leaned his head back against the grime encrusted wall, raising his face to the light, his hair had the glint of bright chestnut, a gold which was also red. And for his swamper's labor he was almost fastidiously clean.

"You—Lansor!"

He shivered as if an icy wind had found him and opened his eyes. They seemed disproportionately large in his skin and bone face and were of an odd shade, neither green nor blue, but somewhere between.

"Get going, you! Ain't paying out good credits for you to sit there like you was buying on your own!" The Salarkian who loomed above him spoke accentless, idiomatic Basic Space which came strangely from between his yellow lips. A furred hand thrust the handle of a mop-up stick at the young man, a taloned thumb jerked the direction in which to use that evil-smelling object. Vye Lansor levered himself up the wall, took the mop, setting his teeth grimly.

Someone had spilled a mug of Kardo and the deep purple liquid was already patterning the con-stone floor past any hope of cleaning. But he set to work slapping the fringe of the noisome mop back and forth to sop up what he could. The smell of the Kardo uniting with the general effluvia of the room and its inhabitants heightened his queasiness.

Working blindly in a half stupor, he was not aware of the man sitting alone in the booth until his mop spattered the ankle of one of the drinking girls. She struck him sharply

13

across the face with a sputtering curse in the tongue of Al-
tar-Ishtar.

The blow sent him back against the open lattice of the
booth. As he tried to steady himself another hand reached
up, fingers tightened about his wrist. He flinched, tried to
jerk away from that hold, only to discover that he was the
other's prisoner.

And looking down at his captor in apprehension, he was
aware even then of the different quality of this man. The
patron wore the tunic of a crewman, lighter patches where
the ship's badges should have been to show that he was not
engaged. But, though his tunic was shabby, dirty, his magnetic boots scuffed and badly worn, he was not like the
others now enjoying the pleasures of the Starfall.

"This one—he makes trouble?" The vast bulk of the Vorm-
man who was the Starfall's private law moved through the
crowd with serene confidence in his own strength, which
no one there, unless blind, deaf, and out-of-the-senses drunk,
could dispute. His scaled, six-fingered, claw hand reached
out for Lansor and the boy cringed.

"No trouble!" There was the click of authority in the voice
of the man in the booth. His face, moments earlier taut and
sharp with intelligence, was suddenly slack, his tone slurred
as he answered: "Looks like an old shipmate. No trouble,
just want a drink with an old shipmate."

But the grip which had pulled Vye forward, swung him
around and down on the other bench in the booth, was anything but slack. The Vorm-man glanced from the patron of
the Starfall to its least important employee and then grinned,
thrusting its fanged jaws close to Lansor's

"If the master wants to drink, you dirt-rat, you drink!"

Vye nodded vigorously, and then put his hand to his
mouth, afraid his stomach was about to betray him again.
Apprehensive, he watched the Vorm-man turn away. Only
when that broad, green-gray back was lost in the smoky
far reaches of the room did he expel his breath again.

"Here—" The grip was gone from his wrist, but fingers
now put a mug into his hand. "Drink!"

He tried to protest, knew it was hopeless, and used both
hands to get the mug to his lips, mouthing the stinging liquid in dull despair. Only, instead of bringing nausea with
it, the stuff settled his stomach, cleared his head, with an

after glow with which he managed to relax from the tense state of endurance which filled his hours in the Starfall.

Half of the mug's contents inside him and he dared to raise his eyes to the man opposite him. Yes, this was no common crewman, nor was he drunk as he had pretended for the Vorm-man. Now he watched the milling crowd with a kind of detachment, though Vye was sure he was aware of every move he himself made.

Vye finished the liquid. For the first time since he had come into this place two months earlier he felt like a real person again. And he had wits enough to guess that the potion he had just swallowed contained some drug. Only now he did not care at all. Anything which could wipe out in moments all the shame, fear, and sick despair the Starfall had planted in him was worth swallowing. Why the other had drugged him was a mystery, but he was content to wait for enlightenment.

Lansor's companion once more applied that compelling pressure to the younger man's bony forearm. Linked by that hold they left the Starfall, came into the cooler, far more pleasant atmosphere of the street. They were a block away before Vye's guide halted, though he did not release his prisoner.

"Forty names of Dugor!" he spat.

Lansor waited, breathing in the air of early morning. The confidence of the drug still held. At the moment he was certain nothing could be as bad as the life behind him, he was willing to face what this strange patron of the Starfall had in mind.

The other slapped his hand down on an air-car call button, stood waiting until one of the city flitters landed on beam before them.

From the seat of the air-car Vye noted they were heading into the respectability of the upper city, away from the stews ringing the launch port. He tried to guess their destination or purpose, not that either mattered much. Then the car descended on a landing stage.

The stranger waved Lansor through a doorway, down a short corridor into a room of private quarters. Vye sat down gingerly on the foam seat extending from the wall as he neared. He stared about. Dimly he could just remember rooms which had this degree of comfort, but so dimly now he could not be sure they did not exist only in his vivid imagination. For Vye's imagination had buoyed him first through the drab existence in a State Child's Créche, then through a state-found job which he had lost because he could not adapt to the mechanical life of a computer tender, and had been an anchor and an escape when he had sunk through the depths of the port to the last refuge in the Starfall.

Now he pressed both his hands into the soft stuff of the seat and gaped at a small tri-dee on the wall facing him, a miniature scene of life on some other planet wherein a creature enveloped in short black and white striped fur crept belly flat, to stalk long-legged, short-winged birds making blood-red splotches against yellow reed banks under a pale violet sky. He feasted on its color, on the sense of freedom and off-world wonders which it raised in him.

"Who are you?"

The stranger's abrupt question brought him back, not only to the room but to his own precarious position. He moistened his lips, no longer quite so aglow with confidence.

"Vye—Vye Lansor." Then he added his other identification, "S. C. C. 425061."

"State child, eh?" The other had pushed a button for a refresher cup, then was sipping its contents slowly. He did not ring for a second to offer Vye. "Parents?"

Lansor shook his head. "I was brought in after the Five-Hour Fever epidemic. They didn't try to keep records, there were too many of us."

The man was watching him levelly over the rim of that cup. There was something cold in that study, something which curbed Vye's pleasant feeling of only moments earlier. Now the other set down his drink, crossed the room. Cupping his hand under Lansor's chin, he brought up his head in a way which stirred a sullen resentment in the younger man, yet something told him resistance would only bring trouble.

"I'd say Terran stock—not more than second generation." He was talking to himself more than to Vye. He loosed his hold on the boy's chin, but he still stood there surveying him from head to foot. Lansor wanted to squirm, but he fought that impulse, and managed to meet the other's gaze when it reached his face again.

"No—not the usual port-drift. I was right all the way."

16

Now he looked at Vye again as if the younger man did have a brain, emotions, some call on his interest as a personality. "Want a job?"

Lansor pressed his hand deeper into the foam seat. "What —*what* kind?" He was angry and ashamed at that small betraying break in his voice.

"You have scruples?" The stranger appeared to think that amusing. Vye reddened, but he was also more than a little surprised that the man in the worn space uniform had read hesitancy right. Someone out of the Starfall should not be too particular about employment, and he could not tell why he was.

"Nothing illegal, I assure you." The man crossed to set his refresher cup in the empty slot. "I am an Out-Hunter."

Lansor blinked. This had all taken on some of the fantastic aura of a dream. The other was eyeing him impatiently, as if he had expected some reaction.

"You may inspect my credentials if you wish."

"I believe you," Vye found his voice.

"I happen to need a gearman."

But this wasn't happening! Of course, it couldn't happen to him, Vye Lansor, state child, swamper in the Starfall. Things such as this did not happen, except in a thaline dream, and he wasn't a smoke eater! It was the kind of dream a man didn't want to wake from, not if he was port-drift.

"Would you be willing to sign on?"

Vye tried to clutch reality to himself, to remain levelheaded. A gearman for an Out-Hunter! Why five men out of six would pay a large premium for a chance at such rating. The chill of doubt cut through the first hazy rosiness. A swamper from a port-side dive simply did not become a gearman for a Guild Hunter.

Again it was as if the stranger read his thoughts. "Look here," he spoke abruptly. "I had a bad time myself, years ago. You resemble someone to whom I owe a debt. I can't repay him, but I can make the scales a little even this way."

"Make the scales even." Vye's fading hope brightened. Then the Out-Hunter was a follower of the Fata Rite. That would explain everything. If you could not repay a good deed to the one you owed, you must balance the Eternal Scales in another fashion. He relaxed again, a great many of his unasked questions so answered.

17

"You will accept?"

Vye nodded eagerly. "Yes, Out-Hunter." He still could not believe that this was happening.

The other pressed the refresher button, and this time he handed Lansor the brimming cup. "Drink on the bargain." His words had the ring of command.

Lansor drank, gulping down the contents of the cup, and suddenly was aware of being tired. He leaned back against the wall, his eyes closed.

Ras Hume took the cup from the lax fingers of the young man. So far, very good. Chance appeared to be playing on his side of the board. It had been chance which had steered him into the Starfall just three nights ago when he had been in quest of his imposter. And Vye Lansor was better than he dared hope to find. The boy had the right coloring, he had been batted around enough to fall for the initial story, he was malleable now. And after Wass' techs worked on him he would be Rynch Brodie—heir to one-third of Kogan-Bors-Wazalitz!

"Come!" He touched Vye on the shoulder. The boy opened his eyes but his gaze did not focus as he got slowly to his feet. Hume glanced at his planet-time watch. It was still very early; the chance he must run in getting Lansor out of this building was small if they went at once. Guiding the younger man with a light hold above the elbow, he walked him out back to the flitter landing stage. The air-car was waiting. Hume's sense of being a gambler facing a run of good luck grew as he shepherded the boy into the flitter, punched a cover destination and took off.

On another street he transferred himself and his charge into a second air-car, set the destination to within a block of the address Wass had given him. Not much later he walked Vye into a small lobby with a discreet list of names posted in its rack. No occupations attached to those colored streamers Hume noted. This meant either that their owners represented luxury trades, where a name signified the profession or service, or that they were covers—perhaps both. Wass' world fringed many different circles, intermingled with some quite surprising professions dedicated to the comfort, pleasure or health of the idle rich, off-world nobility, and the criminal elite.

Hume fingered the right call button, knowing that the

thumb pattern he had left on Wass' conference table would have already been relayed as his symbol of admission here. A flicker of light winked below the name, the wall to the right shimmered, and produced a doorway. Steering Vye to it, Hume nodded to the man waiting there. He was a flat-faced Eucorian of the servant caste, and now he reached out to draw Lansor over the threshold.

"I have him, gentlehomo." His voice was as expressionless as his face. There was another shimmer and the door disappeared.

Hume brushed his hand down the outer side of his thigh, wiping flesh against the coarse stuff of the crew uniform. He left the lobby frowning at his own thoughts.

Stupid! A swamper from one of the worst rat holes in the port. Like as not that youngster would have had his brains kicked out in a brawl, or been fried to a crisp when some drunk got wild with a blaster, before the year was out. He'd done him a real kindness, given him a chance at a future less than one man in a billion ever had the power to even dream about. Why, if Vye Lansor had known what was going to happen to him, he would have been so willing to volunteer, that he would have dragged Hume here. There was no reason to have any regrets over the boy, he had never had it so good—never! There was only one small period of risk for Vye to face. Those days he would have to spend alone on Jumala between the time Wass' organization would plant him there and the coming of Hume's party to "discover" him. Hume himself would tape every possible aid to cover that period. All the knowledge of a Guild Out-Hunter, added to the information gathered by the survey, would be used to provide Rynch Brodie with the training necessary for wilderness survival. Hume was already listing the items to be included as he strode down the street, his tread once more assured.

3

HIS HEAD ached dully, of that he was conscious first. As he turned, without opening his eyes, he felt the brush of softness against his cheek, and a pungent odor fill his nostrils.

He opened his eyes, stared up past a rim of broken rock toward the cloudless, blue-green sky. A relay clicked into proper place deep in his mind.

Of course! He had been trying to lure a strong-jaws out of its traphole with hooked bait, then his foot had slipped. Rynch Brodie sat up, flexed his bare thin arms, and moved his long legs experimentally. No broken bones, anyway. But still he frowned. Odd—that dream which jarred with the here and now.

Crawling to the side of the creek, he dipped head and shoulders into the water, letting the chill of the stream flush away some of his waking bewilderment. He shook himself, making the drops fly from his uncovered torso and arms, and then discovered his hunting tackle.

He stood for a moment fingering each piece of his scanty clothing, recalling every piece of labor or battle which had added pouch, belt, strip of fabric to his equipment. Yet—there was still that odd sense of strangeness, as if none of this was really his.

Rynch shook his head, wiped his wet face with his arm. It was all his, that sure, every bit of it. He'd been lucky, the survival manual on the L-B had furnished him with general directions and this was a world which was not unfriendly —not if one was prepared for trouble.

He climbed up and loosened the net, coiling its folds into one hand, taking the good spear in his other. A bush stirred ahead, against the pull of the light breeze. Rynch froze, then the haft of his spear slid into a new hand grip, the coils of his net spun out. A snarl cut over the purr of water.

The scarlet blot which sprang for his throat was met with the flail of the net. Rynch stabbed twice at the creature he had so swept off balance. A water-cat, this year's cub. Dying, its claws, over-long in proportion to its paws, drew inch deep furrows in the earth and gravel. Its eyes, almost the same shade as its long, burr-entangled body fur, glared up at him in deathly enmity.

As Rynch watched, that feeling that he was studying something strange, utterly alien, came to him once again. Yet he had hunted water-cats for many seasons. Fortunately they were solitary, evil-tempered beasts that marked out a roaming territory to defend it from others of their kind, and not too many were to be encountered in cross-country travel.

He stooped to pull his net from the now still paws. Some definite place he must reach. The compulsion to move on in that sudden flash shook him, raised the dull ache still troubling his temples into a punishing throb. Going down on his knees, Rynch once more turned to the stream water; this time after splashing it onto his face, he drank from his cupped hands.

Rynch swayed, his wet hands over his eyes, digging fingertips into the skin of his forehead to ease that pain bursting in his skull. Sitting in a room, drinking from a cup—it was as if a shadow picture fitted over the reality of the stream, rocks and brush about him. He had sat in a room, had drank from a cup—that action had been important!

A sharp, hot pain made him lose contact with that shadow. He looked down. From the gravel, from under rocks, gathered an army of blue-black, hard-shelled things, their clawed forelimbs extended, blue sense organs raised on fleshy stalks well above their heads, all turned towards the dead feline.

Rynch slapped out vigorously, stumbled into the water loosening the hold of two vicious scavengers on the torn skin of his ankle when he waded out knee-deep. Already that black tongue of small bodies licked across the red-haired side of the hunter. Within minutes the corpse would be only well-cleaned bones.

Retrieving his spear and net, Rynch immersed both in the

water to clean off attackers, and hurried on, splashing through the creek until he was well away from the vicinity of the kill. A little later he flushed a four-footed creature from between two rocks and killed it with one blow from his spear haft. He skinned his kill, feeling the substance of the skin. Was it exceedingly rough hide, or rudimentary scales? And knew a return of that puzzlement.

He felt, he thought painfully as he toasted the dry looking, grayish meat on a sharpened stick, as if a part of him knew very well what manner of animal he had killed. And yet, far inside him, another person he could not understand stood aloof watching in amazement.

He was Rynch Brodie, and he had been traveling on the Largo Drift with his mother.

Memory presented him automatically with a picture of a thin woman with a narrow, rather unhappy face, a twist of elaborately dressed hair in which jeweled lights sparkled. There had been something bad—memory was no longer exact but chaotic. And his head ached as he tried to recall that time with greater clarity. Afterwards the L-B and a man with him in it—

"Simmons Tait!"

An officer, badly hurt. He had died when the L-B landed here. Rynch had a clear memory of himself piling rocks over Tait's twisted body. He had been alone then with only the survival manual and some of the L-B supplies. The important thing was that he must never forget he was Rynch Brodie.

He licked grease from his fingers. The ache in his head made him drowsy. He curled up on a patch of sun-warmed sand and slept.

Or did he? His eyes were open again. Now the sky above him was no longer a bowl of light, but rather a muted halo of evening. Rynch sat up, his heart pounding as if he had been racing to outdistance the rising wind now pushing against his half-naked body.

What was he doing here? Where *was* here?

Panic, carried through from that awakening, dried his mouth, roughened his skin, made wet the palms of the hands he dug into the sand on either side of him. Vaguely, a picture projected into his mind—he had sat in a room, and watched a man come to him with a cup. Before that, he had been in a place of garish light and evil smells.

But he was Rynch Brodie, he had come here on an L-B when he was a boy, he had buried the ship's officer under a pile of rocks, managed to survive by himself because he had applied the aids in the boat to learn how. This morning he had been hunting a strong-jaw, tempting it out of its hiding by a hook and line and a bait of fresh killed skipper.

Rynch's hands went to his face, he crouched forward on his knees. That all was true, he could prove it—he would prove it! There was the strong-jaw's den back there, somewhere on the rise where he had left the snapped haft of the spear he had broken in his fall. If he could find the den, then he would be sure of the reality of everything else.

He had only had a very real dream—that was it! Only, why did he continue to dream of that room, that man, and the cup? Of the place of lights and smells, which he hated so much that the hate was a sour taste in his fright-dried mouth? None of it had ever been a part of Rynch Brodie's world.

Through the dusk he started back up the stream bed, towards the narrow little valley where he had wakened after that fall. Finally, finding shelter within the heart of a bush, he crouched low, listening to the noises of another world which awoke at night to take over the stage from the day dwellers.

As he plodded back, he fought off panic, realizing that some of those noises he could identify with confidence, while others remained mysteries. He bit down hard on the knuckles of his clenched fist, attempting to bend that discovery into evidence. Why did he know at once that that thin, eerie wailing was the flock call of a leather-winged, feathered tree dweller, and that a coughing grunt from downstream was just a noise?

"Rynch Brodie—Largo Drift—Tait." He tasted the blood his teeth drew from his own skin as he recited that formula. Then he scrambled up. His feet tangled in the net, and he went down again, his head cracking on a protruding root.

Nothing tangible reached him in that brush shelter. What did venture out of hiding to investigate was a substance none of his species could have named. It was neither body, nor mind—perhaps it was closest to alien emotion.

Making contact stealthily, but with confidence, it explored after its own fashion. Then, puzzled, it withdrew to report. And since that to which it reported was governed by a set pattern which had not been altered for eons, its only answer was a basic command reaffirmed. Again it made contact, strove to carry out that order fruitlessly. Where it should have found easy passage, a clear channel to carry influence to the sleeper's brain, it found a jumble of impressions, interwoven until they made a protective barrier.

The invader strove to find some pattern, or meaning—withdrew baffled. But its invasion, as ghostly as that had been, loosened a knot here, cleared a passage there.

Rynch awoke at dawn, slowly, dazedly, sorting out sounds, smells, thoughts. There was a room, a man, trouble and fear, then there was he, Rynch Brodie, who had lived in this wilderness on an unmapped frontier world for the passage of many seasons. That world was about him now, he could feel its winds, hear its sounds, taste, smell. It was not a dream—the other was the dream. It had to be!

Prove it. Find the L-B, retrace the trail of yesterday past the point of the fall which had started all this. Right there was the slope down which he must have tumbled. Above, he would find the den he had been exploring when the accident had occurred.

Only—he did not find it. His mind had produced a detailed picture of that rounded depression, at the bottom of which the strong-jaw lurked. But when he reached the crown of the bluff, nowhere did he sight the mounded earth of the pit's rim. He searched carefully for a good length, both north and south. No den—no trace of one. Yet his memory told him that there had been one here yesterday.

Had he fallen elsewhere and stumbled on, dazed, to fall a second time?

Some disputant inside him said no to that. This was where he had regained consciousness yesterday and there was no den!

He faced away from the river, breathing fast. No den— was there also no L-B? If he had passed this way dazed from a former fall, surely he would have left some trace.

There was a crushed, browned plant flattened by weight. He stooped to finger the wilted leaves. Something had come in this direction. He would back-track. Rynch gave a hunter's attention to the ground.

A half-hour later he found nothing but some odd, almost obliterated marks on grass too resilient to hold traces very long. And from them he could make nothing.

He knew where he was, even if he did not know how he got here. The L-B—if it did exist—was to the west. He had a vivid mental picture of the rocket shape, its once silvery sides dulled by exposure, canted crookedly amid trees. And he was going to find it!

Beyond the edge of any conscious sense there was a new stir. He was contacted again, tested. A forest called delicately in its alien way. Rynch had a fleeting thought of trees, was not aware of more than a mild desire to see what lay in their shade.

For the present his own problem held him. That which beckoned was defeated, repulsed by his indifference. While Rynch started at a steady distance to trot towards the east, far away a process akin to a relay clicked into a second set of impulse orders.

Well above the planet Hume spun a dial to bring in the image of the wide stretches of continents, the small patches of seas. They would set down on the western land mass. Its climate, geographical features and surface provided the best site. And he had the very important co-ordinates for their camp already taped in the directo.

"That's Jumala."

He did not glance around to see what effect that screen view had on the other four men in the control cabin of the safari ship. Just now he was striving to master his impatience. The slightest hint could give birth to a suspicion which would blast their whole scheme. Wass might have had a hand in the selection of the three clients, but they would certainly be far from briefed on the truth of any discovery made on Jumala—they had to be for the safety of the whole enterprise.

The fourth man, serving as his gearman for this trip, was Wass' own insurance against any wrong move on Hume's part. And the Out-Hunter respected him as being man enough to be wary of giving any suspicion of going counter to the agreed plan.

Dawn was touching up the main points of the western continent, and he must set this spacer down within a day's journey of the abandoned L-B. Exploration in that direction would be the first logical move for his party. They could not be openly steered to the find, but there were ways of directing a hunt which would do as well.

Two days ago, according to schedule, their castaway had been deposited here with a sub-conscious command to remain in the general area. There had been a slight element of risk in leaving him alone, armed only with the crude weapons he could manipulate, but that was part of the gamble.

They were down—right on the mark. Hume saw to the unpacking and activating of those machines and appliances which would protect and serve his civ clients. He slapped the last inflate valve on a bubble tent, watched it critically as it billowed from a small roll of fabric into a weather resistant, one-room, air-conditioned and heated shelter.

"Ready and waiting for you to move in, Gentlehomo," he reported to the small man who stood gazing about him with a child's wondering interest in the new and strange.

"Very ingenious, Hunter. Ah—now just what might that be?" His voice was also eager as he pointed a finger to the east.

4

HUME GLANCED up alertly. There was a bare chance that "Brodie" might have witnessed their arrival and might be coming in now to save them all a great amount of time and trouble by acting the overjoyed, rescued castaway.

But he could sight nothing at all in that direction to excite any attention. The distant mountains provided a stark, dark blue background. Up their foothills and lower slopes was a thick furring of trees with foliage of so deep a green as to register black from this distance. And on the level country was the lighter blue-green of the other variety of wood edging the open country about the river. In there rested the L-B.

"I don't see anything!" he snapped, so sharply the little man stared at him in open surprise. Hume forced a quick smile.

"Just what did you sight, Gentlehomo Starns? There is no large game in the woodlands."

"This was not an animal, Hunter. Rather a flash of light, just about there." Again he pointed.

Sun, Hume thought, could have been reflected from some portion of the L-B. He had believed that small spacer so covered with vines and ringed in by trees that it could not have been so sighted. But a storm might have disposed of some of nature's cloaking. If so Starns' interest must be fed, he would make an ideal discoverer.

"Odd." Hume produced his distance glasses. "Just where, Gentlehomo?"

"There." Starns obligingly pointed a third time.

If there had been anything to see it was gone now. But it did lie in the right direction. For a second or two Hume was uneasy. Things seemed to be working too well; his cynical distrust was triggered by fitting so smoothly.

"Might be the sun," he observed.

"Reflected from some object you mean, Hunter? But the flash was very bright. And there could be no mirror surface in there, surely there could not be?"

Yes, things were moving too fast. Hume might be overly cautious but he was determined that no hint of any preknowledge of the L-B must ever come to these civs. When they would find the Largo Drift's life boat and locate Brodie, there would be a legal snarl. The castaway's identity would be challenged by a half dozen distant and unloving relatives, and there would be an intense inquiry. These civs must be the impartial witnesses.

"No, I hardly believe in a mirror in an uninhabited forest, Gentlehomo," he chuckled. "But we are on a hunting planet and not all its life forms have yet been classified."

"You are thinking of an intelligent native race, Hunter?"

Chambriss, the most demanding of the civ party, strode up to join them.

Hume shook his head. "No native intelligence on a hunting world, Gentlehomo. That is assured before the planet is listed for a safari. However, a bird or flying thing, perhaps with metallic plumage or scales to catch the sunlight, might under the right circumstances seem a flash of light. That has happened before."

"It was *very* bright," Starns said doubtfully. "We might look over there later."

"Nonsense!" Chambriss spoke briskly as one used to overriding the conflicting wishes in any company. "I came here for a water-cat, and a water-cat I'm going to have. You don't find those in wooded areas."

"There will be a schedule," Hume announced. "Each of you has signed up, according to contract, for a different trophy. You for a water-cat, Gentlehomo. And you, Gentlehomo Starns, want to make tri-dees of the pit-dragons. While Gentlehomo Yactisi wishes to try electo fishing in the deep holes. To alternate days is the fair way. And, who knows, each of you may discover your own choice near the other man's stake out."

"You are quite right, Hunter," Starns nodded. "And since my two colleagues have chosen to try for a water creature, perhaps we should start along the river."

It was two days, then, before they could work their way into the woods. One part of Hume protested, the more cautious section of his mind was appeased. He saw, beyond the three clients now turning over and sorting space bags, Wass' man glanced at the woods and then back to Starns. And, being acutely aware of all undercurrents here, Hume wondered what the small civ had actually seen.

The camp was complete, a cluster of seven bubble tents not too far from the ship. At least this crowd did not appear to consider that the Hunter was there to do all the serious moving and storing of supplies. All three of the clients pitched in to help, and Wass' man went down to the river to return with half a dozen silver-fins cleaned and threaded on a reed, ready to broil over the cook unit.

A fire in the night was not needed except to afford the proper stage setting. But it was enjoyed. Hume leaned forward to feed the flames, and Starns pushed some lengths of driftwood closer.

"You have said, Hunter, that hunting worlds never contain intelligent native life. Unless the planet is minutely explored how can your survey teams be sure of that fact?" His voice bordered on the pedantic, but his interest was plain.

"By using the verifier." Hume sat crosslegged, his plastahand resting on one knee. "Fifty years ago, we would have had to keep rather a lengthy watch to be sure of a free world. Now, we plant verifiers at suitable test points. Intelligence means mental activity of some sort—any of which would be recorded on the verifier."

"Amazing!" Starns extended his plump hands to the flames in the immemorial gesture of a human attracted not only to the warmth of the burning wood, but to its promise of security against the forces of the dark. "No matter how few, or how scattered your native thinkers may be, you record them without missing any?"

Hume shrugged. "Maybe one or two," he grinned, "might get through such a screening. But we have yet to discover a planet with such a sparse native life as that at the level of intelligence."

Yactisi juggled a cup in and out of the firelight. "I agree, this is most interesting." He was a thin man, with scanty drab gray hair and dark skin, perhaps the result of the mingling of several human races. His eyes were slightly sunken, so that it was difficult in this light to read their expression. He was, Hume had already decided, a class one brain and observant to a degree, which could either be a help or a menace. "There have been no cases of failure?"

"None reported," Hume returned. All his life he had relied on machines operating, of course, under the competent domination of men trained to use them properly. He understood the process of the verifier, had seen it at work. At the Guild Headquarters there were no records of its failure; he was willing to believe it was infallible.

"A race residing in the sea now—could you be sure your machine would discover its presence?" Starns continued to question.

Hume laughed. "Not to be found on Jumala, you may be sure of that—the seas here are small and shallow. Such, not to be picked up by the verifier, would have to exist at great depths and never venture on land. So we need not fear any surprises here. The Guild takes no chances."

"As it always continues to assure one," Yactisi replied. "The hour grows late. I wish you rewarding dreams." He arose to go to his own bubble tent.

"Yes, indeed!" Starns blinked at the fire and then scrambled up in turn. "We hunt along the river, then, tomorrow?"

"For water-cat," Hume agreed. Of the three, he believed Chambriss the most impatient. Might as well let him pot his trophy as soon as possible. The ex-pilot deduced there would be little cooperation in exploration from that client until he was satisfied in his own quest.

Rovald, Wass' man, lingered by the fire until the three civs were safe in their bubbles.

"River range tomorrow?" he asked.

"Yes. We can't rush the deal."

"Agreed." Rovald spoke with a curtness he did not use when the civs were present. "Only don't delay too long. Remember, our boy's roaming around out there. He might just be picked off by something before these stumble-footed civs catch up with him."

"That's the chance we knew we'd have to take. We don't dare raise any suspicion. Yactisi, for one, is no fool, neither is Starns. Chambriss just wants to get his water-cat, but he could become nasty if anyone tried to steer him."

"Too long a wait might run us into trouble. Wass doesn't like trouble."

Hume spun around. In the half light of the fire his features were set, his mouth grim. "Neither do I, Rovald, neither do I!" he said softly, but with an icy promise beneath the words.

Rovald was not to be intimidated. He grinned. "Set your fins down, fly-boy. You need Wass—and I'm here to hold his stakes for him. This is a big deal, we won't want any misses!"

"There won't be any—not from my side." Hume stepped away from the fire, approached a post which gleamed with a dull, red line of fire down either side. He pressed a control button. That red line flared into a streak of brilliance. Now encircling the bubble tents and the space ship was a force field: routine protection of a safari camp on a strange world and one Hume had set as a matter of course.

He stood for a long moment staring through that invisible

barrier toward the direction of the wood. It was a dark night, there were scudding clouds to hide the stars, which meant rain probably before morning. This was no time to be plagued by uncertain weather.

Somewhere out there Brodie was holed up. He hoped the boy had long ago reached the "camp" so carefully erected and left for his occupancy. The L-B, that stone covered "grave" showing signs of several years' occupancy, was all assembled and constructed to the last small detail. Far less might have deceived the civs in this safari. But as soon as the story of their find leaked, there would be others on the scene, men trained to assess the signs of a castaway's fight for survival. His own Guild training and the ability of Wass' renegade techs should bring them through that test.

What had Starns seen? The glint of sun on the tail of the L-B, tilted now to the sky? Hume walked slowly back to the fire, when he saw Rovald going up the ramp into the spacer. He smiled. Did Wass think he was stupid enough not to guess that the Veep's man would be in com touch with his employer? Rovald was about to report along some channel of the shadow world that they had landed and that the play was about to begin. Hume wondered idly how far and through how many relays that message would pass before it reached its destination.

He stretched and yawned, moving to his sleeping pad. Tomorrow they must find Chambriss a water-cat. Hume shoved Brodie into the back of his mind to center his thoughts on the various ways of delivering, to the waiting sportsman, a fair-sized alien feline.

The lights in the bubbles went out one by one. Within the circle barrier of the force field men slept. And by midnight the rain began to fall, streaming down the sides of the bubbles, soaking the ashes of the fire.

Out of the dark crept that which was not thought, not substance, but alien to the off-world men. But the barrier, meant to deter mul i-footed creatures, with wings or no visible limbs at all, proved to be a better protection than its creators had hoped. There was no penetration—only a baffled butting of one force against another. And then the probe withdrew as undetected as it had come.

Only, the thing which had no intelligence, as humankind rated intelligence, did possess the ability to fathom the nature of that artificial barrier. The force field was examined, its nature digested. First approach had failed. The second was now ready—ready as it had not been months before when the first coming of these creatures had alerted the very ancient watchdog on Jumala.

Deep in the darker woods on the mountain sides there was a stirring. Things whimpered in their sleep, protested subconsciously commands they could never understand, only obey. With the coming of dawn there would be a marshaling of hosts, a new assault—not on the camp, but on any leaving its protection. And also on the boy now sleeping in a shallow cave formed by the swept roots of a tree—a tree which had crashed when the L-B landed.

Again, fortune favored Hume. With the dawn the rain was over. There was a cloudy sky overhead, but he believed the day would clear. The roily, rushing water of the river would aid Chambriss' quest. Water-cats holed up in the banks, but rising water often forced them out of such dens. A coarse parallel to the stream bed could well show them the tracks of one of the felines.

They started off in a group, Hume leading, with Chambriss treading briskly behind him, Rovald bringing up the rear in the approved trail technique. Chambriss carried a needler, Starns was unarmed except for a small protection stunner, his tri-dee box slung on his chest by well-worn carrying straps. Yactisi shouldered an electric pole, wore its control belt buckled about his middle, though Hume had warned him that the storm would prevent any deep hole fishing.

Only a short distance from the campsite they came upon the unmistakable marks of a water-cat's broad paws, pressed in so heavy and distinct a pattern that Hume knew the animal could not be far ahead. The indentations were deep, and he measured the distance between them with the length of his hand.

"Big one!" Chambriss exclaimed in satisfaction. "Going away from the river, too."

That point puzzled Hume slightly. The red coated felines might be washed out of their burrows, but they did not willingly head so sharply away from the water. He squatted on his heels and surveyed the stretch of countryside between them and the distant wood with care.

The grass was this season's, still growing, not tall enough to afford cover for an animal with paws as large as these prints. There were two clumps of brush. It could have holed up in either, waiting to attack any trailer—but why? It had not been wounded, nor frightened by their party, there was no reason for it to set an ambush on its back trail.

Starns and Yactisi dropped back, though Starns was fussing with his tri-dee. Rovald caught up. He had drawn his ray tube in answer to Hume's hand wave. Any action foreign to the regular habits of an animal was to be mistrusted.

Getting to his feet Hume paced along the line of marks. They were fresh—hot fresh. And they still led in a straight line for the woods. With another wave of his hand he stopped Chambriss. The civ was trained in spite of his eagerness and obeyed. Hume left the tracks, made a detour which brought him to a point from which he could study those clumps of brush. No sign except that line of prints pointed to the woods. And if the party kept on, they might well come upon the L–B!

He decided to risk it. But when they were less than a couple of yards from the tree fringe his hand shot up to direct Chambriss to fire towards the quivering bush.

Only, that formless half seen thing, hardly to be distinguished in color from the vegetation, was no water-cat. There was a thin, ragged cry. Then the creature plunged backward, was gone.

"What in the name of nine Gods was that?" Chambriss demanded.

"I don't know." Hume went forward, jerked the needler dart from a tree trunk. "But don't shoot again—not unless you are sure of what you are aiming at!"

5

MOISTURE FROM the night's rain hung on the tree leaves, clung in globules to Rynch's sweating body. He lay on a wide branch trying to control the heavy panting which supplied his laboring lungs. And he could still hear the echoes of the startled cries which had come from the men who had threaded through the woods to the up-pointed tail fins of the L-B.

Now he tried to reason why he had run. They were his own kind, they would take him out of the loneliness of a world heretofore empty of his species. But that tall man— the one who had led the party into the irregular clearing about the life boat—

Rynch shivered, dug his nails into the wood on which he lay. At the sight of that man, dream and reality had crashed together, sending him into panic-stricken flight. That was the man from the room—the man with the cup!

As his heart quieted he began to think more coherently. First, he had not been able to find the strong-jaws's den. Then the marks on the ground at the point from which he had fallen and the L-B were here, just as he remembered. But not far from the small ship he had discovered something more—a campsite with a shelter fashioned out of spalls and vines, containing possessions a castaway might have accumulated.

That man would come, Rynch was sure of that, but he was too spent to struggle on.

No, the answer to every part of the puzzle lay with that man. To go back to the ship clearing was to risk capture— but he had to know. Rynch looked with more attention at his present surroundings. Deep mold under the trees here

34

would hold tracks. There might just be another way to move. He eyed the spread of limbs on a neighbor tree.

His journey through those heights was awkward and he sweated and cringed when he disturbed vocal treetop dwellers. He was also to discover that close to the site of the L-B crash others waited.

He huddled against the bole of a tree when he made out the curve of a round bulk holding tight to the tree trunk aloft. Though it was balled in upon itself he was sure the creature was fully as large as he, and the menacing claws suggested it was a formidable opponent.

When it made no move to follow him Rynch began to hope it had only been defending its own hiding place, for its present attitude suggested concealment.

Still facing that featureless blob in the tree, the man retreated, alert for the first sign of advance on the part of the creature above. None came, and he dared to slip around the bole of the tree under which he stood, listening intently for any corresponding movement overhead. Now he was facing that survivor's camp.

Another object crouched in the dark of the lean-to shelter, just as its fellow was on sentry duty in the tree! Only this one did not have the self-color of the foliage to disguise it. Four-limbed, its long forearms curved about its bent knees, its general outline almost that of a human—if a human went clothed in a thick fuzz. The head hunched right against the shoulders as if the neck were very short, or totally lacking, was pear-shaped, with the longer end to the back, and the sense organs of eyes and nose squeezed together on the lower quarter of the rounded portion, with a line of wide mouth to split the blunt round of the muzzle. Dark pits for eyes showed no pupil, iris, or cornea. The nose was a black, perfectly rounded tube jutting an inch or so beyond the cheek surface. Grotesque, alien and terrifying, it made no hostile move. And, since it had not turned its head, he could not be sure it had even sighted him. But it knew he was there, he was certain of that. And was waiting—for what? As the long seconds crawled by Rynch began to believe that it was not waiting for him. Heartened, he pulled at the vine loop, climbed back into the tree.

Minutes later he discovered that there were more than two of the beasts waiting quietly about the camp, and that their sentry line ran between him and the clearing of the L-B. He withdrew farther into the wood, intent upon finding a detour which would bring him out into the open lands. Now he wanted to join forces with his own kind, whether those men were potential enemies or not.

As time passed the beasts closed about the clearing of the camp. Afternoon was fading into evening when he reached a point several miles downstream near the river. Since he had come into the open he had not sighted any of the watchers. He hoped they did not willingly venture out of the trees where the leaves were their protection.

Rynch went flat on the stream bank, made a worm's progress up the slope to crouch behind a bush and survey the land immediately ahead. There stood an off-world spacer, fins down, nose skyward, and grouped not too far from its landing ramp, a collection of bubble tents. A fire burned in their midst and men were moving about it.

Now that he was free from the wood and its watchers and had come so near to his goal, Rynch was curiously reluctant to do the sensible thing, to rise out of concealment and walk up to that fire, to claim rescue by his own kind.

The man he sought stood by the fire, shrugging his arms into a webbing harness which brought a box against his chest. Having made that fast he picked up a needler by its sling. By their gestures the others were arguing with him, but he shook his head, came on, to be a shadow stalking among other shadows. One of the men trailed him, but as they reached a post planted a little beyond the bubble tents he stopped, allowed the explorer to advance alone into the dark.

Rynch went to cover under a bush. The man was heading to the stream bed. Had they somehow learned of his own presence nearby, were they out to find him? But the preparations the tall man had made seemed more suited to going on patrol. The watchers! Was the other out to spy on them? That idea made sense. And in the meantime he would let the other past him, follow along behind until he was far enough from the camp so that his friends could not interfere—then, they would have a meeting!

Rynch's fingers balled into fists. He would find out what was real, what was a dream in this crazy, mixed up mind of his! That other would know, and would tell him the truth!

Alert as he was, he lost sight of the stranger who melted into the dusky cover of the shadows. Then came a quiet ripple of water close to his own hiding place. The man from the spacer camp was using the stream as his road.

In spite of his caution Rynch was close to betrayal as he edged around a clump of vegetation growing half in, half out of the stream. Only a timely rustle told him that the other had sat down on a drift log.

Waiting for him? Rynch froze, so startled that he could not think clearly for a second. Then he noted that the outline of the other's body was visible, growing brighter by the moment.

Minute particles of pale-greenish radiance were gathering about the other. The dark shadow of an arm flapped, the radiance swirled, broke again into pinpoint sparks.

Rynch glanced down at his own body—the same sparks were drifting in about him, edging his arms, thighs, chest. He pushed back into the bushes while the sparks still flitted, but they no longer gathered in strength enough to light his presence. Now he could see they drifted about the vegetation, about the log where the man sat, about rocks and reeds. Only they were thicker about the stranger as if his body were a magnet. He continued to keep them whirling by means of waving hand and arm, but there was enough light to show Rynch the fingers of his other hand, busy on the front panel of the box he wore.

That fingering stopped, then Rynch's head came up as he heard a very faint sound. Not a beast's cry—or was it? Again those fingers moved on the panel. Was the other sending a message by that means? Rynch watched him check the webbing, count the equipment at his belt, settle the needler in the crook of his arm. Then the stranger left the stream, headed towards the woods.

Rynch jumped to his feet, a cry of warning shaping, but not to be uttered. He padded after the other. There was plenty of time to stop the man before he reached the danger which might lurk under the trees.

However the other was as wary of that dark as if he suspected what might lie in wait there. He angled along northward, avoiding clumps of scattered brush, keeping in the open where Rynch dared not tail him too closely.

Their course, parallel to the woods, brought them at last

to a second stream, the size of a river, into which the first creek emptied. Here the other settled down between two rocks with every indication of remaining there for a period.

Thankfully Rynch found his own lurking place from which he could keep the other in sight. The light points gathered, hung in a small luminous cloud over the rocks. But Rynch had prudently withdrawn under a bush, and the scent of its aromatic leaves must have discouraged the sparks, for no such crown came to his sentry post.

Drugged with fatigue, the younger man slept, awaking to full day, a fog of bewilderment and disorientation. To open his eyes to this blue-green pocket instead of to four dirty walls, was wrong.

Remembering, he started up and slunk down the slope, angry at his failure. He found the other's track, not turning back as he had half feared, cleanly printed on level spots of wet earth—eastward now. What was the purpose of the other's expedition? Was he going to use the open cut through which the river ran as a way of penetrating the wooded country?

Now Rynch considered the problem from his own angle. The man from the spacer had made no effort to conceal his trail, in fact it would almost seem that he had deliberately gone out of his way to leave boot prints on favorable stretches of ground. Did he guess that Rynch lurked behind, was now leading him on for some purpose of his own? Or were those traces left to guide another party from the camp?

To advance openly up the stream bed was to invite discovery. Rynch surveyed the nearer bank. Clumps of small trees and high growing bushes dotted that expanse, an ideal cover.

He was hardly out of sight of the bush which had sheltered him when he heard the coughing roar of a water-cat. And the feline was attacking an enemy, enraged to the pitch of vocal frenzy. Rynch ran a zig-zag course from one clump of bush to the next. That sound of snarling, spitting hate ended in mid-cry as Rynch crawled to the river bank.

The man from the spacer camp had been the focus of a three-prong attack from a female and her cubs. Three red bodies were flat and still on the gravel as the off-worlder leaned back against a rock breathing heavily. As Rynch sighted him, he stooped to recover the needler he had dropped, lurched away from the rock towards the water, and so blundered straight into another Jumalan trap.

His unsteady foot advancing for another step came down on a slippery surface, and he fell forward as his legs were engulfed in the trap burrow of a strong-jaws. With a startled cry the man dropped the needler again, clawed at the ground about him. Already he was buried to his knees, then his mid-thighs, in the artificial quicksand. But he had not lost his head and was jerking from side to side in an effort to pull free.

Rynch got to his feet, walked with slow deliberation down to the river's brink. The trapped prisoner had shied halfway around, stretching out his arms to find a firmer grip on some rock large and heavy enough to anchor him. After his first startled cry he had made no sound, but now, as he sighted Rynch, his eyes widened and his lips parted.

The box on his chest caught on a stone he had dragged to him in a desperate try for support. There was a spitting of sparks and the stranger worked frantically at the buckle of the webbing harness to loosen it and toss the whole thing from him. The box struck one of the dead water-cats, flashed as fur and flesh were singed.

Rynch watched dispassionately before he caught the needler, jerking it away from the prisoner. The man eyed him steadily, and his expression did not alter even when Rynch swung the off-world weapon to center its sights on the late owner.

"Suppose," Rynch's voice was rusty sounding in his own ears, "we talk now."

The man nodded. "As you wish, Brodie."

6

"Brodie?" Rynch squatted on his heels.

Those gray eyes, so light in the other's deeply tanned face, narrowed the smallest fraction, Rynch noted with an inner surge of triumph.

"Were you looking for me?" he added.

"Yes."

"Why?"

"We found an L-B—we wondered if there were survivors."

Slowly Rynch shook his head. "No—you knew I was here. Because you brought me!" He fashioned his suspicions into one quick thrust.

This time there was not the slightest hint of self-betrayal from the other.

"You see," Rynch leaned forward, but still well out of reach from the captive, "I remember!"

Now there was a faint flicker of answer in the man's eyes. He asked quietly:

"What do you remember, Brodie?"

"Enough to know that I am not Brodie. That I did not get here on the L-B, did not build that camp."

He ran one hand over the stock of the needler. Whatever motive lay behind this weird game into which he had been unwillingly introduced, he was now sure that it was serious enough to be dangerous.

"You have no cup this time."

"So you do remember." The other accepted that calmly. "All right. That need not necessarily spoil our plans. You have nothing to return to on Nahuatl—unless you *liked* the Starfall." His voice was icy with contempt. "To play our roles will be for your advantage, too." He paused, his gaze centering on Rynch with the intensity of one willing the desired answer out of his inferior.

Nahuatl. Rynch caught at that. He had been on or in Nahuatl—a planet? a city? If he could make this man believe he remembered everything clearly, more than just the scattered patches that he did . . .

"You had me planted here, then came back to hunt me. Why? What makes Rynch Brodie so important?"

"Close to a billion credits!" The man from the spacer leaned well back in the hole, his arms spread flat out on either side to keep his body from sinking deeper. "A billion credits," he repeated softly.

Rynch laughed. "You'll have to think of a better one that that, fly-boy."

"The stakes would have to be high, wouldn't they, for us to go to all this staging? You've been conditioned, Brodie, illegally brain-channeled!"

To Rynch the words meant nothing. If they ever had, that was gone, lost in the maze of other things which had been blotted out of his mind by the Brodie past. But he would not give the other the advantage of knowing his uncertainty.

"You need a Brodie for a billion credits. But you don't have a Brodie now!"

To his surprise the prisoner in the earth trap laughed. "I'll have a Brodie when he's needed. Think about a good share of a billion credits, boy, keep thinking of that hard."

"I will."

"Thoughts alone won't work it, you know." For the first time there was a hint of some emotion in the man's voice.

"You mean I need you? I don't think so. I've stopped being a plaque for someone to play across the board." That expression brought another momentary flash of hazy memory—a smoky, crowded room where men slid counters back and forth across tables—not one of Brodie's edited recalls, but his own.

Rynch stood up, started for the rise of the slope, but before he topped that he glanced back. The damaged com box still smoked where its wearer had flung it. Now the man was already straining forward with both arms, trying to reach a rock just a finger space beyond. Lucky for him the burrow was an old one, uninhabited. In time he should be able to work his way out. Meanwhile there was the whole of a wide countryside in which Rynch could discover a hideout—no one would find him now against his will.

He tried, as he strode along, to piece together more of his memories and the scanty information he had had from the Nahuatl man. So he had been "brain-channeled," given a set of false memories to fit a Rynch Brodie whose presence on this world meant a billion credits for someone. He could not believe that this was the spaceman's game alone, for hadn't he spoken of "we"?

A billion credits! The sum was fantastic, the whole story unbelievable.

There was a hot stab of pain on his instep. Rynch cried out, stamped hard. One of the clawed scavengers was crushed. The man leaped back in time to avoid another step into a swarming mass of them at work on some unidentifiable carrion. Staring down at the welter of scaled, segmented bodies and busy claws, he gasped.

41

Three dead water-cats were near the man trapped in the pit. Bait to draw these voracious eaters straight to the prisoner. Rynch's empty stomach heaved. He swung around, ran across the grassy verge of the upper bank, hoping he was not too late.

As he half fell, half slid down to the water, he saw that the man had managed to hook the webbing of the smouldering box to him, was casting it out and dragging it back patiently, aiming at the nearest rock of size, fruitlessly attempting to hitch its straps over the round of stone.

Rynch dashed on, caught at that loop of webbing, and dug his heels into the loose gravel as he began a steady pull. With his aid the other crawled out, lay panting. Rynch grabbed the man's shoulder, jerked him away from the body of the female water-cat. He was sure he had seen a telltale scurrying around the smaller of the dead cubs.

The man straightened, glanced toward Rynch who was backing off, the needler up and ready between them.

"My turn to ask why?"

Then his gaze followed Rynch's. The smallest cub twitched from side to side. Not with any faint trace of life, but under the attack of the scavengers. More scuttled towards the second cub.

"Thanks!" The stranger was on his feet. "My name is Ras Hume. I don't think I told you that when we last met."

"This doesn't make any difference. I'm not your man, not Brodie!"

Hume shrugged. "You think about it, Brodie, think about it with care. Come back to camp with me and—"

"No!" Rynch interrupted. "You go your way, I go mine from here on."

Again the other laughed. "Not so simple as all that, boy. We've started something which can't just be turned off as easily as you snap down a switch." He took a step or two in Rynch's direction.

The younger man brought up the needler. "Stay right where you are! Your game, Hume? All right, you play it—but not with me."

"And what are you going to do, take to the woods?"

"What I do is my business, Hume."

"No, my business, too, very much so. I'm giving you a warning, boy, in return for your help here." He nodded at the pit. "There's something in that woods—something which didn't show up when the Guild had their survey exploration here."

"The watchers." Rynch retreated step by step, keeping the needler ready. "I saw them."

"You've seen them!" Hume was eager. "What do they look like?"

In spite of his desire to be rid of Hume, Rynch found himself answering that in detail, discovering that on demand he could recall minutely the description of the animal hiding in the tree, the one who had waited in the shelter, and those he had glimpsed drawing in about the L-B clearing.

"No intelligence." Hume turned his head to survey the distant wood. "The verifier reported no intelligence."

"These watchers—you don't know them?"

"No. Nor do I like what you've seen of them, Brodie. So I'm willing to call a truce. The Guild believed Jumala an open planet, our records accredited it so. If that is not true we may be in for bad trouble. As an Out-Hunter I am responsible for the safety of three civs back there in the safari camp."

Hume made sense, much as Rynch disliked admitting it. And the Hunter must have read something of his agreement in his face for now he nodded and added briskly:

"Best place now is the safari camp. We'll head back at once."

Only time had run out. A noise sounded with a metallic ring. Rynch whirled, needler cocked. A glittering ball about the size of his fist rolled away from contact with a boulder, came to rest in the deep depression of one of Hume's boot tracks. Then another flash through the air, a clatter as a second ball spun across a patch of gravel.

The balls seemed to appear out of the air. Displaying rainbow glints they rolled in a semicircle about the two men. Rynch stooped, then Hume's fingers latched about his wrist, dragging his hand away from the globe. It was only then that he realized that sharp action had detached his attention from that ball he had wanted to take up.

"Don't touch!" Hume barked. "And don't look at that too closely! Come along!" He pulled Rynch forward through the yet unclosed arc of the globe circle.

Hume detoured around the feasting scavengers and

43

brought Rynch with him at a trot. They could hear behind them the plop and tinkle of more globes. Glancing back Rynch saw one fall close to the bodies of the water-cats.

"Wait a minute!" He pulled back against Hume's hold. Here was a chance to see what effect that crystal had on the clawed carrion eater.

There was a change in the crystal: Yellow now, then red—red as the few scraps of fur remaining on the rapidly disappearing body.

"Look!"

The pulsating carpet which had covered the dead feline ceased to move. But towards that spot rolled two more of the globes, approaching the scavengers. Now the clawed things were stirring, dropping away from their prey. They spread out in a patch, moved purposefully forward. Behind them, as guardians might head a flock, rolled three globes, flushing scarlet, then more.

Hume's hand came up. From the cone tip of the ray tube spat a lance of fire, to strike the middle crystal. The beam was reflected into the block of scavengers. Scaled bodies, twisted, crisped, were ash. But the crystal continued to roll at the same pace.

"Move!" Hume's other hand hit Rynch's shoulder, knocked him forward in an impetuous shove which nearly took him off his feet. Both men began to run.

"What—what are those things?" Rynch appealed between panting breaths.

"I don't know—and I don't like their looks. They're between us and the safari camp if we keep to the river—"

"Between us and the river now." Rynch saw that glittering swoop through the air, marked the landing of a ball near the water's edge.

"Might be trying to box us in. But that's not going to work. See—ahead there where that log's caught between two rocks? Run out on that when we reach there and take to the water. I don't think those things can float and if they sink to the bottom that ought to fix them as far as we are concerned."

Rynch ran, still holding the needler. He balanced along the drift log Hume had pointed out and a jump sent him floundering in the brown stream thigh deep. Hume joined him, his face grim.

"Downstream—"

Rynch looked. One shape—two—three— Clearly detailed where matching vegetation gave them no covering camouflage, the watchers had come out of the woods at last. A line of them were walking quietly and upright towards the humans, their blue-green fuzz covering like a mist under the direct rays of the sun. Quiet as they seemed at present, the things out of the Jumalan forest were a picture of sheer brute strength as they moved.

"Let's get out of here—fast!"

The men kept moving, and always after them padded that silent line of green-blue, pushing them farther and farther away from the safari camp, on towards the rising mountain peaks. Just as the globes had shaken the scavengers loose from their meal and sent them marching on, so were the humans being herded for some unknown purpose.

At least, once the march of the beasts began, they saw and heard no more of the globes. And as they reached a curve in the river, Hume stopped, swung around, stood studying the line of decorously pacing animals.

"We can pick them off with the needler or the ray."

The Hunter shook his head. "You don't kill," he recited the credo of his Guild, "not until you are sure. There is a method behind this, and method means intelligence."

Handling of X-tee creatures and peoples was a part of Guild training. In spite of his devious game here on Jumala, Hume was Guild educated and Rynch was willing to leave such decisions to him.

The other held out the ray tube. "Take this, cover me, but don't use it until I say so. Understand?"

He waited only for Rynch's nod before he started, at a deliberate pace which matched that of the beasts, back through the river shallows to meet them. But that advancing line halted, stood waiting in silence. Hume's hands went up, palm out, he spoke slowly in Basic-X-Tee clicks:

"Friend." This was all Rynch could make out of that singsong of syllables Rynch knew to be a contact pattern.

The dark eye pits continued to stare. A light breeze ruffled the fuzz covering of wide shoulders, long muscular arms. Not a head moved, not one of those heavy, rounded jaws opened to emit any answering sound. Hume halted. The silence was threatening, a portending atmosphere spread from the alien things as might a tangible wave.

For perhaps two breaths they stood so, man facing alien. Then Hume turned, walked back, his face set. Rynch offered him the ray tube.

"Fight our way out?"

"Too late. Look!"

Moving lines of blue-green coming down to the river. Not five or six now—a dozen—twenty. There was a small trickle of moisture down the side of the Hunter's brown face.

"We're penned—except straight ahead."

"But we're going to fight!" Rynch protested.

"No. Move on!"

7

IT WAS some time before Hume found what he wanted, an islet in midstream lacking any growth and rising to a rough pinnacle. The sides were seamed with crevices and caves which promised protection for one's back in any desperate struggle. And they had discovered it none too soon, for the late afternoon shadows were lengthening.

There had been no attack, just the trailing to herd the men to the northeast. And Rynch had lost the first tight pinch of panic, though he knew the folly of underestimating the unknown.

They climbed with unspoken consent, going clear to the top, where they huddled together on a four-foot tableland. Hume unhooked his distance lenses, but it was toward the rises of the mountains that he aimed them, not along the back trail.

Rynch wriggled about, studied the river and its banks. The beasts there were quiet, blue-green lumps, standing down on the river bank or squatting in the grass.

"Nothing." Hume lowered the lenses, held them before his broad chest as he still watched the peaks.

"What did you expect?" Rynch snapped. He was hungry, but not hungry enough to abandon the islet.

Hume laughed shortly. "I don't know. Only I'm sure they are heading us in that direction."

"Look here," Rynch rounded on him. "You know this planet, you've been here before."

"I was one of the survey team that approved it for the Guild."

"Then you must have combed it pretty thoroughly. How is it that you didn't know about them?" He gestured to their pursuers.

"That is what I would like to ask a few assorted experts right about now," Hume returned. "The verifiers registered no intelligent native life here."

"No native life." Rynch chewed that over, came up with the obvious explanation. "All right—so then maybe our blue-backed friends are imported. Suppose someone's running a private business of his own here and wants to get rid of visitors?"

Hume looked thoughtful. "No." He did not enlarge upon his negative. Sitting down he pulled a cylinder container from a belt loop and shook out four tablets, handing two to Rynch, mouthing the others.

"Vita-blocks—good for twenty-four hours sustenance."

The iron rations depended upon by all exploring services did not have the satisfying taste of real food. However Rynch swallowed them dutifully before he descended with Hume to river level. The Hunter splashed water from the stream into a depression in the rock and dropped a pinch of clarifying powder into it.

"With the dark," he announced, "we might be able to get through their lines."

"You believe that?"

Hume laughed. "No—but one doesn't overlook the factor of sheer luck. Also, I don't care to finish up at the place they may have chosen for us." He tilted his chin to study the sky. "We'll take watches and rest in turn. No use trying anything until it is dark—unless they start to move in. You take the first one?"

As Rynch nodded, Hume edged back into a crevice as a shelled creature withdrawing to natural protection, going to sleep as easily as if he could control that state by will.

Rynch, watching him curiously for a second or two before climbing up to a position from which he judged he could see all sides of their refuge, determined not to be surprised.

The watchers were crouched down, waiting with that patience which had impressed him from his first sight of the camp sentries back in the forest. There was no movement, no sound. They were simply there—on guard. And Rynch did not believe that the darkness of night would bring any relaxation of that vigilance.

He leaned back, feeling the grit of the rocky surface against his bare back and shoulders. Under his hand was the most efficient and formidable weapon known to the frontier worlds, from this post he could keep the enemy under surveillance and think.

Hume had had him planted here, in the first place, provided with the memory of Rynch Brodie—the reward for him was to be a billion credits. Too much staff work had gone into his conditioning for just a small stake.

So Rynch Brodie was on Jumala, and Hume had come with witnesses to find him. Another part of his mind stood aloof now, applauding the clearness of his reasoning. Rynch Brodie was to be discovered a castaway on Jumala. Only, matters had not worked out according to Hume's plan. In the first place he was certain he had not been intended to know that he was *not* Rynch Brodie. For a fleeting second he wondered why that conditioning had not completely worked, then went back to the problem of his relationship with Hume.

No, the Out-Hunter had expected a castaway who would be just what he ordered. Then this affair of the watchers—creatures the Guild men had not found here a few months ago—Rynch felt a small cold chill along his spine. Hume's game was one thing, something he could understand, but the silent beasts were another and somehow far more disturbing threat.

Rynch edged forward, watching the mist on the water, his brain striving to solve this other puzzle as neatly as he thought he had discovered the reason for his scrambled memories and his being on Jumala.

The mist was an added danger. Thick enough and those watchers could move in under its curtain. A needler was efficient, yes, but it could wipe out only an enemy at which

48

it was aimed. Blind cross sweeping with its darts would only exhaust the clip without results, save by lucky chance.

On the other hand, suppose they could turn that same gray haze to their own advantage—use it to blanket their withdrawal? He was about to go to Hume with that suggestion when he sighted the new move in their odd battle with the aliens.

A wink of light—two more—blinking, following the erratic course by the pull of the stream. All bobbing along toward the rugged coastline of the islet. Those had appeared out of nothingness as suddenly as the globes when this chase had begun.

The globes and the winking lights on the water connected in his mind, argued new danger. Rynch took careful aim, fired a dart at one which had grounded on the pointed tip of the rocks where the river current came together after its division about the island. For the first time Rynch realized those things below were moving *against* the current—they had come upsteam as if propelled.

He had fired and the light was still there, two more coming in behind it, so that now there was an irregular cluster of them. And there was activity on the water-washed rocks before them. Just as the scavengers had moved ahead of the globes on land, so now aquatic creatures had come out of the river, were flopping higher on the islet. And those lights were changing color—from white to reddish-yellow.

Lynch scrabbled with one hand in a rock crevice, found a stone he had noted earlier. He hurled that at the cluster of lights. There was a puff of brilliant red, one was gone. Something flopping on the rocks gave a mewling cry and somersalted back into the water. Then a finger of mist drew between Rynch and the lights which were now only faint, glowing patches. He swung down from his perch, shook Hume awake.

The Out-Hunter made that instant return to full consciousness which was another defense for the men who live long on the rim of wild worlds.

"What—?"

Rynch pulled him forward. The mist had thickened, but there were more of those ominous lights at water level, spreading down both sides of the point, forming a wall. Dark forms moved out of the water ahead of them, flopping on the rocks, pressing higher, towards the ledge where the men stood.

"Those globes—I think they're moving in the river now." Rynch found another stone, took careful aim, and smashed a second one. "The needler has no effect on them," he reported. "Stones do—but I don't know why."

They searched about them in the crevices for more ammunition, laying up a line of fist-sized rocks, while the lights gathered in, spreading farther and farther down the shores of the islet. Hume cried out suddenly, and aimed his ray tube below. The lance of its blast cut the dark as might a bolt of lightning.

With a shrill squeal, a blot shadow detached from the slope immediately below them. A vile, musky scent, now mingled with the stench of burning flesh, set them coughing.

"Water spider!" Hume identified. "If they are driving those out and up at . . . "

He fumbled at his equipment belt and then tossed an object downward to disintegrate in a shower of fiery sparks. Wherever those sparks touched rock or ground they flared up in tall thin columns of fire, lighting up the nightmare on the rocks and up the ledges.

Rynch fired the needler, Hume's ray tube flashed and flashed again. Things squealed, or grunted, or died silently, while clawing to reach the upper ledges. He could not be sure of the nature of some of those things. One, armed and clawed as the scavengers, was nearly as large as a water-cat. And a furry, man-legged creature, with a double-jawed head, bore also a ring of phosphorescent eyes set in a complete circle about its skull. They were alien life routed out of the water.

"The lights—smash the lights!" Hume ordered.

Rynch understood. The lights had driven these attackers out of the river. Put out the lights and the boiling broth of water dwellers might conceivably return to their homes. He dropped the needler, took up stones and set about the business of finishing off as many of the lights as he could.

Hume fired into the crawling mass, pausing only once to send another of those flame bombs crashing to illuminate the scene. The water creatures bewildered, clumsy out of their element, were so far at his mercy. But their numbers, in spite of the piling dead, were still a dangerous threat.

Rynch tore gapping holes in that line of lights. But he could see, through the mist, more floating sparks, gathering to take their places, perhaps herding before them more water things to attack. Except for those few gaps he had wrought, the islet was now completely enveloped.

"Ahhhh—" Hume's voice arose in a roar of anger and defiance. He stabbed his ray down at a spot just below their ledge. A huge segmented, taloned leg kicked, caught on the edge of the stone at the level of their feet, twisted aloft again and was gone.

"Up!" Hume ordered. "To the top!"

Rynch caught up two handsful of stones, holding them to his chest with his left arm as he made a last cast to see one light puff out in answer. Then they both scrambled on to that small platform at the top of the islet. By the aid of the burning flame-torches the Hunter had set, they could see that most of the rocky slopes below them now squirmed with a horrible mass of water life.

Where Hume had fired his ray there was fierce activity, as the living feasted on the slain and quarreled over the bounty. But from other quarters the crawling advance pressed on.

"I have only one more flame flare," Hume stated.

One more flare—then they would be in the dark with the mist hiding the forward-moving enemy.

"I wonder if they are watching out there?" Rynch scowled into the dark.

"They—or what sent them. They know what they are doing."

"You mean they must have done this before?"

"I think so. That L-B back there—it made a good landing, and there are supplies missing from its lockers."

"Which you removed—" Rynch countered.

"No. There might have been real castaways landed here. Not that we found any trace of them. Now I can guess why—"

"But you Guild men were here, and you didn't run into this!"

"I know." Hume sounded baffled. "Not a sign then."

Rynch threw the last of his stones, heard it clink harmlessly against a rock. Hume balanced an object on the palm of his hand.

51

"Last flare!"

"What's that? Over there?"

Rynch had sighted the flashing out of the dark from the river bank, making a pattern of flickers which bore no relation to the infernal lights at the water's edge.

Hume's ray tube pointed skyward as he answered with a series of short bursts.

"Take cover!" The call came weirdly out over the water, the tone dehumanized. Hume cupped his mouth with one hand, shouted back:

"We're on top—no cover."

"Then flatten down—we're blasting!"

They flattened, lay almost in each other's arms, curled on that narrow space. Even through his closed eyelids Rynch caught the flash of vivid, man-made lightning crashing first on one side of the islet and then on the other, and sweeping every crawling horror out of life, into odorous ash. The backlash of that blast must have caught the majority of the lights also. For when Rynch and Hume cautiously sat up, they saw only a handful of widely scattered and dulling globes below.

They choked, coughed, rubbed watering eyes as the fumes from the scorched rocks wreathed up about their perch.

"Flitter with life line—above you!"

That voice had come out of what should have been empty air over their heads. A gangling line trailed across their bodies, a line with a safety belt locked to it, and a second was uncoiling in a slow loop as they watched.

In unison they grabbed for those means of escape, buckled the belts about them.

"Haul away!" Hume called. The lines tightened, their bodies swung up clear of the blasted river island, as their unseen transport headed for the eastern shore.

8

A SUBDUED but steady light all around him issued from stark gray walls. He lay on his back in an empty cell-room. And he'd better be on the move before Darfu comes to enforce a rising order with a powerful kick or one of these backhanded blows which the Salarkian used to reduce most humans to helpless obedience.

Vye blinked again. But this wasn't his cubby hole at the Starfall, his nose as well as his eyes told him that. There was no hint of uncleanliness or corruption here. He sat up stiffly, looked down at his own body in dull wonder. The only covering on his bare, brown self was a wide, scaled belt and a loin cloth. Clumsy sandals shod his feet, and his legs, up to thigh level, were striped with healing scratches and blotched with bruises.

Painfully, with mental processes as stiff as his arms and his legs, he tried to think back. Sluggishly, memory associated one picture with another.

Last night—or yesterday—Rynch Brodie had been locked in here. And "here" was one of the storage compartments of a spacer belonging to a man named Wass. It had been Wass' pilot in the flitter which snaked them from the river islet where the monsters had beseiged them.

This was a concealed, fortified camp—Wass' hide-out. And he was a prisoner with a very uncertain future, depending upon the will of the Veep and a man named Hume.

Hume, the Out-Hunter, had shown no surprise when Wass stood up in the lamplight to greet the rescued. "I see you have been hunting." His eyes had moved from Hume to Rynch and back again.

"Yes—but that does not matter!" the Hunter had returned impatiently.

"No? Then what does?"

"This is not a free world, I have to report that. Get my civs off planet before something happens to them!"

"I thought all safari worlds were certified as free," Wass countered.

"This one isn't. I don't know how or why. But that fact has to be reported and the civs lifted—"

"Not so fast." Wass' voice had been quiet, almost gentle. "Such a report would interest the Patrol, would it not?"

"Of course—" Hume began and then stopped abruptly. Wass smiled. "You see—complications already. I do not wish to explain anything to the Patrol. Nor do you either, my young friend, not when you stop to think about what might result from such explanations."

"There wouldn't have been any trouble if you'd kept away from Jumala." Hume's control had returned; both voice and manner were under tight rein. "Weren't Rovald's reports explicit enough to satisfy you?"

"I have risked a great deal on this project," Wass replied. "Also, it is well from time to time for a Veep to check upon his field operatives. Men do not grow careless when personal supervision is ever in mind. And it is well that I did arrive here, is it not, Hunter? Or would you have preferred remaining on that island? Whether any of our project may be salvaged is a point we must consider. But for the moment we make no moves. No, Hume, your civs will have to take their chances for a time."

"And if there is trouble?" Hume challenged him. "A report of an alien attack will bring in the Patrol quickly enough."

"You forget Rovald," Wass corrected. "The chance that one of your civs can activate and transmit from the spacer is remote, and Rovald will see that it is impossible. You have picked up Brodie, I see."

"Yes."

"No!" What had possessed him at that moment to contradict? He had realized the folly of his outburst the moment Wass had looked at him.

"This becomes more interesting," the Veep had remarked with that deceptive gentleness. "You are Rynch Brodie, castaway from the Largo Drift, are you not? I trust that Out-Hunter Hume has made plain to you our concern with your welfare, Gentlehomo Brodie."

"I'm not Brodie." Having taken the leap into the dangerous truth he was stubborn enough to continue swimming.

"I find this enlightening indeed. If you are not Brodie—then who are you?"

That had been it. At that moment he couldn't have told Wass who he was, explain that his patchwork of memories had gaping holes.

"And you, Out-Hunter," Wass' reptilian regard had moved again to Hume, "perhaps you have an adequate explanation for this discovery."

"None of his doing," he burst out, "I remembered—"

Some inexplicable emotion made Rynch defend Hume then.

Hume laughed, and there was a reckless edge to that sound. "Yes, Wass, your techs are not as good as they pretend to be. He didn't follow the pattern of action they set for him."

"A pity. But there are always errors when one deals with the human factor. Peake!" One of the other three men moved towards them. "You will escort this young man to the spacer, see him safely stowed for the present. Yes, a pity. Now we must see just how much can be salvaged."

Then Vye had been brought into the shop, supplied with a ration container, and left to himself within this bare-walled cabin to meditate upon the folly of talking too freely. Why had he been so utterly stupid? Veeps of Wass' calibre did not swim through the murky channels of the Starfall, but their general breed had smaller but just as vicious representatives there, and he knew the man for what he was, ruthless, powerful and thorough.

A sound, slight, but easily heard in the silent vacuum of the storage cabin, alerted him. The crack of the sliding panel door opened and Vye crouched, his hand cupping the only possible weapon, the ration container. Hume edged through, shut the door behind him. He stood there, his head turned so his ear rested against the wall; obviously he was listening.

"You brain-smoothed idiot!" The Hunter's voice was a thread of whisper. "Why couldn't you have kept that swinging jaw of your closed last night? Now listen and listen good. This is a slim try, but it's one we have to take."

"We?" Vye was startled into asking.

"Yes, we! By rights I ought to leave you right here to

do the rest of your big, brave speechmaking for Wass' benefit. If I didn't need you, that's just what I would do! If it
weren't for those civs—" His head snapped back, cheek to
panel, he was listening again. After a long moment his
whisper came once more. "I don't have time to repeat this.
In about five minutes Peake'll be here with rations. I'll leave
this door unlatched. There's another storage cabin across
the corridor—see if you can hide there, then trick him into
getting in here and lock him in. Got it?"

Vye nodded.

"Then—make for the exit port. Here." He snapped a packet
loose from his belt. "This is a flare pak, you saw how they
worked on the island. When you get on the ramp beyond
the atom lamp, throw this. It should hit the camp force barrier. And the result ought to hold their attention. Then you
head for the flitter. Understand?"

"Yes."

The flitter, yes, that was the perfect escape. With a camp
force barrier on, any fugitive could only break out by going
straight up.

Hume gazed at him soberly, listened once more, and then
went. Vye counted a slow five before he followed. The cabin
across the corridor was open, just as Hume had promised.
He slipped inside, waited.

Peake was coming now, the metallic plates on his space-
boots clicking in regular pattern of sound. He carried another ration container and crooked it in his arm as he snapped
up the lock bar on the other cabin.

There was an exclamation of surprise. Vye went into
action. His hand, backed by all the strength of his thrusting
arm, thumped between Peake's shoulders, sending him stag-
gering into the prison compartment. Before the other could
recover either his balance or his wits, Vye had the panel
shut, the bar locked into place.

He ran down the corridor to the well ladder, swung down
its rungs with an agility born of necessity. Then he was in
the air lock, getting his bearings. The flitter stood to his
left, the flashing atom lamp, where the men were gathered,
to his right.

Vye stepped out on the ramp. He wiped his sweating
hand across his thigh. There had to be no failures in the
tossing of the flare pak.

Choosing a spot, not directly in line with the lamp but near enough to dazzle the men, he hurled it with all the force he could muster. Then he was running down the ramp, forward to the area of the ship.

There was a flash—shouting—Vye curbed the impulse to look back, darted for the flitter. He jerked open the cabin compartment, scrambled into the cramped space behind the pilot's seat, leaving that free for Hume's quick entrance. More shouting—now he saw the lines of fire wavering from earth to sky along the barrier.

A black shape put on a burst of speed, was silhouetted against that flaming wall, then passed the spacer, grabbed at the open cockpit, and slid in behind the controls. Hume pulled the levers with flying fingers. They arose vertically at a pace which practically slapped Vye's stomach up into the lower regions of his throat.

The searing line of at least one blaster reached after them—too slowly, too low. He heard Hume grunt, and they again leaped higher. Then the Hunter spoke:

"Half an hour at the most—"

"The safari camp?

"Yes."

They no longer climbed. The flitter was boring forwards on a projectile flight, into the dark of the night.

"What're those?" Vye suddenly leaned forward.

Had some of the stars across the space void broken free from their fixed orbits? Flecks of light, moving in an arc, headed towards the speeding flitter.

Hume hit a button. Again they arose in a violent leap above those wandering lights. But ahead on this new level more such dots flocked, moving fast to close in on the flyer.

"A straight ram course," Hume muttered, more to himself than Vye.

Again the flyer drove forward in a rising thrust of speed. Then the smooth purr of the propulsion unit faltered, broke into protesting coughs. Hume worked over the controls, beads of sweat showing on his forehead and cheek in the gleam of the cabin light.

"Deading—deading out!"

He brought the flitter around in a wide circle, the purr smoothed out once more in a steady reassuring beat.

"Out run them!"

But Vye feared they were back again on the losing side of a struggle with the unknown alien power. As they had been herded along the river, so now they were being pushed across the sky, towards the mountains. The enemy had followed them aloft!

Some core of stubborn will in Hume would not yet allow him to admit that. Time and time again he climbed higher—always to meet climbing, twisting, spurting lines of lights which reacted on the engine of the flitter and threatened it with complete failure.

Where they were now in relation to Wass' camp or that of the safari, Vye had no idea, and he guessed that Hume could not be too certain.

Hume switched on the flitter's com unit, tried a channel search until he picked up a click of signal—the automatic reply of the safari camp. His fingertip beat out in return the danger warning, then the series of code sounds to give an edited version of what must be guarded against.

"Wass has a man in your camp. His skin is in just as much danger as the rest. He may not relay it to the Patrol, but he'll keep the force barrier up and the civs inside—anything else would be malicious neglect and a murder charge when the Guild check tape goes in. This call is on the spacer tape now and will be a part of that—he can't possibly alter such a report and he knows it. This is the best we can do now—"

"We're close to the mountains, aren't we?"

"Do you know much about this part of the country?" Vye persisted. Hume's knowledge might be their only hope.

"Flew over the range twice. Nothing to see."

"But there has to be something there."

"If there is, it didn't show up during our survey." Hume's voice was dull with fatigue.

"You're a Guild man, you've dealt with alien life forms before—"

"The Guild doesn't deal with intelligent aliens. That's X-Tee Patrol business. We don't land on any planet with unknown intelligent life forms. Why should we court trouble—couldn't run a safari in under those conditions. X-Tee certified Jumala as a wild world, our survey confirmed that."

"Someone or something landed here after you left?"

"I don't believe so. This is too well organized an action. And since we have a satellite guard in space, any ship landing would be taped and recorded. No such record appeared on the Guild screens. One small spacer—such as Wass'—could slip through by knowing procedure—just as he did. But to land all those beasts and equipment they'd need a regular transport. No—this must be native." Hume leaned forward again, flipped a switch.

A small red light answered on the central board.

"Radar warn-off," he explained.

So they wouldn't end up smeared against some cliff face anyway. Which was only small comfort amid terrifying possibilities.

Hume had taken the precaution just in time. The light blinked faster, and the speed of the flyer was checked as the automatic control triggered by the warn-off came into command. Hume's hands were still on the board, but a system of relays put safety devices into action with a speed past that which a human pilot could initiate.

They were descending and had to accept that, since the warn-off, operating for the sake of the passengers, had ruled that move best. The directive would glide the flitter to the best available landing. It was only moments before the shock gear did touch surface. Then the engine was silent.

"This is it," Hume observed.

"What do we do now?" Vye wanted to know.

"Wait—"

"Wait! For what?"

Hume consulted his planet-time watch in the light of the cabin.

"We have about an hour until dawn—if dawn arrives here at the same time it does in the plains. I don't propose to go out blindly in the dark."

Which made sense. Except that to sit here, quietly, in their cramped quarters, not knowing what might be waiting outside, was an ordeal Vye found increasingly harder to bear. Maybe Hume guessed his discomfort, maybe he was following routine procedure. But he turned, thumbed open one of the side panels in Vye's compartment, and dug out the emergency supplies.

9

THEY SORTED the crash rations into small packs. A blanket of the water-resistant, feather-heavy Ozakian spider silk was cut into a protective covering for Vye. That piece of tailoring occupied them until the graying sky permitted them a full picture of the pocket in which the flitter had landed. The dark foliage of the mountain growth was broken here by a ledge of dark-blue stone on which the flyer rested.

To the right was a sheer drop, and a land slip had cut away the ledge itself a few feet behind the flitter. There was only a steadily narrowing path ahead, slanting upward.

"Can we take off again?" Vye hoped to be reassured that such a feat was possible.

"Look up!"

Vye backed against the cliff wall, stared up at the sky. Well above them those globes still swam in unwearied circles, commanding the air lanes.

Hume had cautiously approached the outer rim of the ledge, was using his distance glasses to scan what might lie below.

"No sign yet."

Vye knew what he meant. The globes were overhead, but the blue beasts, or any other fauna those balls might summon, had not yet appeared.

Shouldering their packs they started along the ledge. Hume had his ray tube, but Vye was weaponless, unless somewhere along their route he could pick up some defensive and offensive arm. Stones had burst the lights of the islet, they might prove as effective against the blue beasts. He kept watch for any of the proper size and weight.

The ledge narrowed, one shoulder scraped the cliff now as

they rounded a pinnacle to lose sight of the flitter. But the globes continued to hover over them.

"We are still traveling in the direction they want," Vye speculated.

Hume had gone to hands and knees to negotiate an ascent so steep he had to search for head and toe holds. When they were safely past that point they took a breather, and Vye glanced aloft again. Now the sky was empty.

"We may have arrived, or are about to do so," said Hume.

"Where?"

Hume shrugged. "Your guess is as good as mine. And both of us can be wrong."

The steep ascent did not quite reach the top of the cliff around the face of which the ledge curled. Instead their path now leveled off and began to widen out so that they could walk with more confidence. Then it threaded into a crevice between two towering rock walls and sloped downward.

A path unnaturally smooth, Vye thought, as if shaped to funnel wayfarers on. And they came out on the rim of a valley, a valley centered with a wood-encircled lake. They stepped from the rock of the passage onto a springy turf which gave elastically to their tread.

Vye's sandal struck a round stone. It started from its bed in the black-green vegetation, turned over so that round pits stared eyelessly up at him. He was faced by the fleshless grin of a human skull.

Hume went down on one knee, examined the ground growth, gingerly lifted the lace of vertabrae forming a spine. That ended in a crushed break which he studied briefly before he laid the bones gently back into the concealing cover of the mossy stuff.

"That was done by teeth!"

The cup of green valley had not changed, it was the same as it had been when they had emerged from the crevice. But now every clump of trees, every wind-rippled mound of brush promised cover.

Vye moistened his lips, diverted his eyes from the skull.

"Weathered," Hume said slowly, "must have been here for seasons, maybe planet years."

"A survivor from the L-B?" Yet this spot lay days of travel from that clearing back in the plains.

"How did he get here?"

"Probably the same way we would have, had we not holed up on that river island."

Driven! Perhaps the lone human on Jumala herded up into this dead-end valley by the globes or the blue beasts. "This process must have been in action for some time."

"Why?"

"I can give you two reasons." Hume studied the nearest trees narrowly. "First—for some purpose, whatever we are up against wants all interlopers moved out of the lowlands into this section, either to imprison them, or to keep them under surveillance. Second—" He hesitated.

Vye's own imagination supplied a second reason, a revolting one he tried to deny to himself even as he put it into words:

"That broken spine—food . . . " Vye wanted Hume to contradict him, but the Hunter only glanced around, his expression already sufficient answer.

"Let's get out of here!" Vye was fighting down panic with every ounce of control he could summon, trying not to bolt for the crevice. But he knew he could not force himself any farther into that sinister valley.

"If we can!" Hume's words lingered direly in his ears. Stones had smashed the globes by the river. If they still waited out there Vye was willing to try and break them with his bare hands, should escape demand such action. Hume must have agreed with those thoughts, he was already taking long strides back to the cliff entrance.

But that door was closed. Hume's foot, raised for the last step toward the crevice corridor, struck an invisible obstruction. He reeled back, clutching at Vye's shoulder.

"Something's there!"

The younger man put out his hand questingly. What his fingers flattened against was not a tight, solid surface, but rather an unseen elastic curtain which gave a little under his prodding and then drew taut again.

Together they explored by touch what they could not see. The crevice through which they had entered was now closed with a curtain they could not pierce or break. Hume tried his ray tube. They watched thin flame run up and down that invisible barrier, but not destroy it.

Hume relooped the tube. "Their trap is sprung."

"There may be another way out!" But Vye was already

despondently sure there was not. Those who had rigged this trap would leave no bolt holes. But because they were human and refused to accept the inevitable without a fight, the captives set off, not down into the curve of the cup, but along its slope.

Tongues of brush and tree clumps brought about detours which forced them slowly downward. They were well away from the crevice when Hume halted, flung up a hand in silent warning. Vye listened, trying to pick up the sound which had alarmed his companion.

It was as Vye strained to catch a betraying noise that he was first conscious of what he did not hear. In the plains there had been squeaking, humming, chitterings, the vocalizing of myriad grass dwellers. Here, except for the sighing of the wind and a few insect sounds—nothing. All inhabitants bigger than a Jumalan fly might have long ago been routed out of the land.

"To the left." Hume faced about.

There was a heavy thicket there, too stoutly grown for anything to lie within its shadow. Whatever moved must be behind it.

Vye looked about him frantically for anything he could use as a weapon. Then he grabbed at the long bush knife in Hume's belt sheath. Eighteen inches of tri-fold steel gleamed wickedly, its hilt fitting neatly into his fist as he held it point up, ready.

Hume advanced on the bush in small steps, and Vye circled to his left a few paces behind. The Hunter was an expert with ray tube; that, too, was part of the necessary skill of a safari leader. But Vye could offer other help.

He shrugged out of the blanket pack he had been carrying on his back, tossed that burden ahead.

Out of cover charged a streak of red, to land on the bait. Hume blasted, was answered by a water-cat's high-pitched scream. The feline writhed out of its life in a stench of scorched fur and flesh. As Vye retrieved his clawed pack Hume stood over the dead animal.

"Odd." He reached down to grasp a still twitching foreleg, stretched the body out with a sudden jerk.

It was a giant of its species, a male, larger than any he had seen. But a second look showed him those ribs starting through mangy fur in visible hoops, the skin tight over the skull, far too tight. The water-cat had been close to death by starvation; its attack on the men probably had been sparked by sheer desperation. A starving carnivore in a land lacking the normal sounds of small birds and animal life, in a valley used as a trap.

"No way out and no food." Vye fitted one thought to another out loud.

"Yes. Pin the enemy up, let them finish off one another."

"But why?" Vye demanded.

"Least trouble that way."

"There are plenty of water-cats down on the plains. All of them couldn't be herded up here to finish each other off; it would take years—centuries."

"This one's capture may have been only incidental, or done for the purpose of keeping some type of machinery in working order," Hume replied. "I don't believe this was arranged just to dispose of water-cats."

"Suppose this was started a long time ago, and those who did it are gone, so now it goes on working without any real intelligence behind it. That could be the answer, couldn't it?"

"Some process triggers into action when a ship sets down on this portion of Jumala, maybe when one planet's under certain conditions only? Yes, that makes sense. Only why wasn't the first Patrol explorer flaming in here caught? And the survey team—we were here for months, cataloguing, mapping, not a whisper of any such trouble."

"That dead man—he's been here a long time. And when did the Largo Drift disappear?"

"Five—six years ago. But I can't give you any answers. I have none."

It began as a low hum, hardly to be distinguished from the distant howling of the wind. Then it slid up scale until the thin wail became an ululating scream torturing the ears, dragging out of hiding those fears of a man confronting the unknown in the dark.

Hume tugged at Vye, drew the other by force back into the brush. Scratched, laced raw by the whip of branches, they stood in a small hollow with the drift of leaves high about their ankles. And the Hunter pulled into place the portions of growth they had dislodged in their passage into the thicket's heart. Through gaps they could see the opening where lay the body of the water-cat.

The wail was cut off short, that cessation in itself a warning. Vye's body, touching earth with knee and hand as he crouched, picked up a vibration. Whatever came towards them walked heavily.

Did the smell of death draw it now? Or had it trailed them from the closed gate? Hume's breath hissed lightly between his teeth. He was sighting the ray tube through a leaf gap.

A snuffling, heavier than a man's panting. A vast blot, which was neither clearly paw nor hand, swept aside leaves and branches on the other side of the small clearing, tearing them casually from the shrubs.

What shuffled into the open might be a cousin of the blue beasts. But where they had given only an impression of brutal menace, this was savagery incarnate. Taller than Hume, but hunched forward in its neckless outline, the thing was a monster. And over the round of the lower jaw, tusks protruded in ugly promise.

Being carnivorous and hungry, it scooped up the body of the water-cat and fed without any prolonged ceremony. Vye, remembering the crushed spine of the human skeleton, was sickened.

Done, it reared on hind feet once again, the pear-shaped head swung in their direction. Vye was half certain he had seen that tube-nose expand to test the air and scent them.

Hume pressed the button of the ray tube. That soundless spear of death struck in midsection of that barrel body. The thing howled, threw itself in a mad forward rush at their bush. Hume snapped a second blast at the head, and the fuzz covering it blackened.

Missing them by a precious foot, the creature crashed straight on through the thicket, coming to its knees, writhing in a rising chorus of howls. The men broke out of cover, raced into the open where they took refuge behind a chimney of rock half detached from the parent cliff. Down the slope the bushes were still wildly agitated.

"What was that?" Vye got out between sobbing breaths.

"Maybe a guardian, or a patrol stationed to dispose of any catch. Probably not alone, either." Hume fingered his ray tube. "And I am down to one full charge—just one."

Vye turned the knife he held around in his fingers, tried to imagine how one could face up to one of those tusked monsters with only this for a weapon. But if that thing had companions, none were coming in answer to its dying wails. And after it had been quiet for a while Hume motioned them out of hiding.

"From now on we'll keep to the open, better see trouble like that before it arrives. And I want to find a place to hole up for the night."

They trailed along the steep upper slope and in time found a place where a now dried stream had once formed a falls. The empty watercourse provided an overhang, not quite a cave, but shelter. Gathering brush and stones, they made a barricade and settled behind it to eat sparingly of their rations.

"Water—a whole lake of it down there. The worst of it is that a water supply in a dry country is just where hunters congregate. That lake's entirely walled in by woodland and provides cover for a thousand ambushes."

"We might find a way out before our water bulbs fail," Vye offered.

Hume did not answer directly. "A man can live for quite a while on very thin rations, and we have tablets from the flitter emergency supplies. But he can't live long without water. We have two bulbs. With stretching that is enough for two days—maybe three."

"We ought to get completely around the cliffs in another day."

"And if we do find a way out, which I doubt, we're still going to need water for the trek out. It's right down there waiting until our need is greater than either our fear or our cunning."

Vye moved impatiently, his blanket-clad shoulders scraping the rock at their backs. "You don't think we have a chance!"

"We aren't dead. And as long as a man is breathing, and on his feet, with all his wits in his skull, he always has a chance. I've blasted off-world with odds stacked high on the other side of the board." He flexed that plasta-flesh hand which was so nearly human and yet not by the fraction which had changed the course of his life. "I've lived on the

66

edge of the big blackout for a long time now—after a while you can get used to anything."

"One thing I would like—to get at the one who set this trap," commented Vye.

Hume laughed with dry humor. "After me, boy, after me. But I think we might have to wait a long time for that meeting."

•

10

VYE CRAWLED weakly from the area of a rock outcrop. The sun, reflected from the cliff side, was a lash of fire across his emaciated body. His swollen tongue moved a pebble back and forth in his dry mouth. He stared dimly down the slope to that beckoning platter of water open under the sun, rimmed with the deadly woodland.

What had happened? They had gone to sleep that first night under the ledge of the dried waterfall. And all of the next day was only a haze to him now. They must have moved on, though he could remember nothing, save Hume's odd behavior—dull-eyed silence while stumbling on as a brainless servio-robot, incoherent speech wherein all the words came fast, running together unintelligibly. And for himself —patches of blackout.

At sometime they had come to the cave and Hume had collapsed, not rousing in answer to any of Vye's struggles to awaken him. How long they had been there Vye could not tell now. He had the fear of being left alone in this place. With water perhaps Hume could be returned to consciousness, but that was all gone.

Vye believed he could scent the lake, that every breeze up slope brought its compelling enticement. Just in case Hume might awake to a state of semi-consciousness and wander off, Vye tethered him with blanket bonds.

Vye fingered Hume's knife, which had been painstakingly lashed to a trimmed shaft of wood. Since he had emerged from that clouding of mind which still gripped the Hunter, he had done what he could to prepare for another attack from any roving beast. And he also had Hume's ray tube—its single charge to be used only in dire need.

Water! His cracked lips moved, ejected the pebble. Their four empty water bulbs were in the front of his blanket tunic, pressing against his ribs. It was now—or die, because soon he would be too weak to make the attempt at all. He darted for the first stand of bush downhill.

As the brooding silence of the valley continued, he reached the edge of the wood unhindered, intent on his mission with a concentration which shut out everything save his need and the manner of satisfying it.

He squatted in the bush, eyeing the length of woodland ahead. Then he tried the only action he had been able to think out. That beast Hume had killed had been too heavy to swing up in trees. But Vye's own weight now did not prohibit that form of travel.

With spear and ray tube firmly attached to him, Vye climbed into the first tree. A slim chance—but his only defense against a possible ambush. A wild outward swing brought him, heart-thudding, to the next set of limbs. Then he had a piece of luck, a looped vine tied together a whole group of branches from one treetop to the next.

Hand grips, balance, sometimes a walk along a branch—he threaded towards the lake. Then he came to a gap. With hands laced into tendrils, Vye hunched to look down on a beaten ribbon of gray earth—a trail well used by the evidence of its pounded surface.

That area had to be crossed on foot, but his passage through the brush below would leave traces. Only—there was no other way. Vye checked the lashings of his weapons again before leaping. Almost in the same instant his sandals hit the packed earth he was running. His palms skinned raw on rough bark as he somehow scrambled aloft once more.

No more vines, but broad limbs shooting well out. He dropped from one to another—stopped for breath—listened. The dark gloom of the wood was broken by sunlight. He was at the final ring of trees. To get to the water he must descend again. A dead trunk extended over the water. If he could run out on that and lower the bulb, it could work.

Eerie silence. No flying things, no tree dwelling reptiles or animals, no disturbance of any water creature on the unruffled surface of the lake. Yet the sensation of life, inimical life, lurking in the depths of the wood, under the water, bore in upon him.

Vye made the light leap to the bole of the dead tree, balanced out on it over the water, moving slowly as the trunk settled a little under his weight. He hunkered down, brought out the first bulb tied fast to a blanket string.

The water of the river had been brown, opaque. But here the liquid was not so cloudy. He could see snags of dead branches below its surface.

And something else!

Down in those turgid depths he made out a straight ridge running with a trueness of line which could not be nature's unassisted product. That ridge joined another in a squared corner. He leaned over, strained his eyes to follow through the murk the farther extent of those two ridges. Looked along both pointed protuberances aimed at the surfaces of the lake, like fangs in an open jaw. Down there was something—something artificially fashioned which might be the answer to all their questions. But to venture into the lake himself—he could not do it! If he could bring the Out-Hunter to his senses the other might find the solution to this puzzle.

Vye filled his bulbs, working speedily, but still studying what he could see of the strange erection under the lake. He thought it was curiously free of silt, and its color, as far as he could distinguish, allowing for the dark hue of the water, was light gray—perhaps even white. He lowered his last bulb.

Down in the bleached forest of dead branches, well to one side of the mysterious walls, there was movement, a slow rolling of a shadow so hidden by a stirring of bottom mud that Vye could not make out its true form. But it was rising to the bulb.

Vye hated to lose a single precious drop. Once he might have the luck to make this journey unmolested, a second time the odds could be too high.

A flash—the slowly rising shadow was transformed into a whizzing spear of attack. Vye snapped the bulb out of the water just as a nightmarish, armored head arose on a whip-lash of coiled, scaled neck, and a blunt nose thudded against the tree trunk with a hollow boom. Vye clung to his perch as the thing flopped back into deeper water from a froth of beaten foam, leaving a patch of odorous scum and slime to bracelet the waterlogged wood.

He ran for the shelter of the trees to get away. This time there was no rear, no thump of feet in warning. Out of the ground itself, or so it seemed to Vye's startled terror, reared one of the tusked beasts. To reach his tree and its dubious safety he had to wind past that chimera. And the creature waited with a semblance of ease for him to come to it.

Vye brought around his spear. The length of the haft might afford him a fighting chance if he could send the point home in some vulnerable spot. Yet he knew that the beasts were hard to kill.

The mouth opened in a wide grin of menace. Vye noted a telltale tightning of shoulder muscles. It was going to rush for him now with those clawed forepaws out to rip.

To wait was to court disaster. Vye shouted, his battle cry piercing the silence of the lake and wood. He sprang, aiming the spear point at the beast's protuberant belly, and then swerved to the side as the knife bit home, raking his weapon to open a gaping wound.

The spear was jerked from Vye's hold as both those taloned paws closed on it. Then the creature pulled it free, snapped the haft in two. Vye fired a short blast from the ray tube before it could turn on him, saw fur-fuzz afire, as he ran for the tree.

Beneath its branches he looked back. The beast was paw-ing at the burning fur on its head, and he had perhaps a second or two. He jumped and his fingers caught on the low hanging branch, then he made a superhuman effort, was up out of the path of the thing which rushed blindly for the tree, shrieking in frenzied complaint.

The huge body crashed against the trunk with force which nearly shook Vye from his hold. As the giant forepaws be-labored the wood, strove to lift the body from the ground, Vye worked his way out on another branch. In the end it was the shaking of that limb under him which aided his swing to the next tree. And from there he traveled recklessly, in-tent only on getting out of the woods as fast as he could.

By the noise the beast was still assaulting the tree, and Vye marveled at its vitality, for the belly wound would long ago have killed any creature he knew. Whether it could trace his flight aloft, or whether its howls would bring more of its kind, he could not guess, but every second he could gain was all important now

At the gap over the trail he hesitated. That path ran in the direction of the open, and to go on foot meant the possibility of greater speed. Vye slipped from the bough, hit the ground, and ran. His ragged lungsful of air came in great gasps and he doubted it he could take the exertion of more tree travel now. He raced down the path.

Those mewling cries were louder, he was sure of it. Now he heard the thump of the beast's blundering pursuit behind him. But its bulk and hurts slowed it. In the open he could find cover behind a rock, use the ray again.

The trees began to thin. Vye summoned power for a last burst of speed, came out of the shadow of the wood as might a dart expelled from a needler. Before him, up slope, was the closed door of the valley. And moving in from the left was another of the blue beasts.

He could not retreat to the trees. But the newcomer was moving with the same ponderous self-confidence its fellow had shown earlier. Vye dodged right, headed for the rocks by the gap. As he pulled himself into that temporary fortification, the wounded beast dragged out of the woods below. He thought it was blind, yet some instinct drove it after him.

Shaking from fatigue, Vye steadied his forearm on the top of the rock, brought up the ray tube. Less than two yards away now was the deceptively open mouth of the gap. If he threw himself at that, would the elasticity of the unseen curtain hurl him back into the claws of the enemy?

He fired his blast at the head of the unwounded beast. It screeched, threw out its arms, and one of those paws struck against its wounded fellow. With a cry, that one flung itself at its companion in the hunt, and they tangled in a body-to-body battle terrible in its utter ferocity. Vye edged along the cliff determined to reach the cave and Hume. And the two blue things seemed intent on finishing each other off.

The one from the wood was done, the fangs of the other ripping out its throat. Tearing viciously the victor made sure of its kill, then its seared head came up, swung about to face Vye. He guessed it was aware of his movements whether it could see or not.

But he was not prepared for the speed of its attacking lunge. Heretofore the creatures had given the impression of brute strength rather than agility. And he had been almost fatally deceived.. He jumped backwards, knowing he must elude that attack, for he could not survive hand-to-hand combat with the alien thing.

There was a moment of dazed disorientation, a weird sensation of falling through unstable space in which there had never been and never would be firm footing again. He was rolling across rock—outside the curtain of the gap.

He sat up, the feeling of being adrift in unmeasurable nothingness making him sick, to watch mistily as the blue beast came to a halt. Whimpering it turned, but before it reached the level of the woods, it sagged to its knees, fell face forward and was still, a destructive machine no longer controlled by life.

Vye tried to understand what had happened. He had somehow broken through that barrier which made the valley a prison. For a moment all that mattered was his freedom. Then he looked apprehensively behind him along the road to the open, more than half expecting to see a gathering of the globes, or of the less impressive lowland beasts that acted as herders. But there was nothing.

Freedom! He dragged himself to his feet. Free to go! He slipped Hume's ray tube back into his belt. Hume was still in the valley!

Vye rubbed his shaking hands across his face. Through the barrier and free—but Hume was back there, without a weapon, defenseless against any questing beast able to nose him out. Sickly, without water and protection, he was a dead man even while he still breathed.

Keeping one hand against the wall of the gap in support, Vye started to walk, not out of the gap towards the distant lowlands, but back into the valley, forcing himself to that by his will alone and screaming inside against such suicidal folly. He put out his hand tentatively when he reached the two points of rock where that curtain had hung. There was no obstruction—the barrier was down! He must get back to Hume.

Still keeping his wall hold, Vye lurched through the gate, was once more in the valley. He stood swaying, listening. But once again there was silence, not even the wind moved through trees or bushes. Placing one foot carefully before the other he went on towards Hume's cave. The haze which had clouded his thinking processes since that first morning's awakening in this bowl was gone now. Except for the physical weakness that weighted his body, he felt once more entirely alive and alert.

Wriggling in the cave's entrance was the Hunter. He had freed the bonds Vye had put on his legs, but his hands were still tied. His face, grimy, sweat-covered, was turned up to the sunlight, and his eyes were again bright with reason.

Vye found the strength to run the last few feet between them. He was fumbling with those ties about Hume's wrists as he blurted out the news. The barrier was out—they could go.

Then he was bringing one of those precious bulbs, raising it to Hume's eager mouth, squeezing a portion of its contents between the man's cracked and bleeding lips.

Somehow they made that trip back to the valley gate. When they saw their goal, Hume broke from Vye's hold, tottered forward with a cry not far removed from a sob. He rebounded to slip full length to the ground and lie there. Sobbing dryly, his gaunt face, eyes closed, turned up to the sky. The trap had snapped shut once again.

"Why—why?" Vye found he was repeating the same words over and over, his gaze blank, unfocussed, yet turned to the woods of the lake.

"Tell me what happened again."

Vye's head came around. Hume had pulled himself up so that his shoulders rested against the rock wall. His plasta-hand was out-flung, slipping up and down what seemed empty air, but which was the barrier against freedom. And now his eyes seemed entirely sane.

Slowly, hesitating between words, Vye went over the full account of his visit to the lake, his retreat before the beasts, his fortunate stumble through the gap.

"But you came back."

Vye flushed. He was not going to try to explain that. Instead he said:

"If it went away once, it can again."

Hume did not press the subject of his return. Rather he fastened upon the end of that action with the wounded beast, made Vye go through it verbally a third time.

"There is just this," he said when the other was done. "When you fell you were not thinking of the barrier at all— and your wits were working again. You had come out of the daze we both had."

Vye tried to remember, decided that the Hunter was correct. He had been trying to elude the charge of the beast, only, fear and that desperate desire had occupied his mind at that moment. But what did that signify?

To test just what he did not know, he crawled now to Hume's side, put up his own hand to the space where the plasta-flesh palm slid back and forth on nothingness. But he almost fell on his face, forward into the gap. Where he had been expecting the resistance of the unseen curtain there had been nothing at all! He turned to Hume with the expression of a man who had been stunned by an unexpected blow.

11

"IT IS OPEN for you!" Hume broke the quiet first. His eyes were very bleak in his bony face.

Vye stood up, took one step and was on the other side of the curtain where Hume's hand still found substance. He came back with the same lack of hindrance. Yes, to him there was no longer a barrier. But why—why him when Hume was still a prisoner?

The Hunter raised his head so his eyes could meet Vye's with the authority of an order. "Go, get away while you can!"

Instead Vye dropped down beside the other. "Why?" he asked baldly. And then the most obvious of all answers came.

He glanced at Hume. The Hunter's head lolled back against

the rock which supported him, his eyes were closed now, and he had the look of a man who had been driven to the edge of endurance and was now willing to relinquish his grip and let go.

Deliberately Vye brought up his right hand, balled his fingers into a fist. And just as deliberately he struck home, square on the point of that defenseless chin. Hume sagged, would have slipped down the surface of the rock had Vye's hands not caught in his armpits.

Since he had not the strength left to get to his feet with such a burden, Vye crawled, dragging the inert body of the Hunter with him. And this time, as he had hoped, there was no resistance at the gap. Unconscious, Hume was able to cross the barrier. Vye stretched him as comfortably flat as he could, used a portion of their water on his face until he moaned, muttered, and raised his hand feebly to his head.

Then those gray eyes opened, focussed on Vye.

"What—"

"We're both through now, both of us!" The younger man saw Hume glance around him with waking belief.

"But how—?"

"I knocked you out, that's how," Vye returned.

"Knocked me out? I crossed when I was unconscious!" Hume's voice steadied, strengthened. "Let me see!" He rolled over on his side, threw out his arm, and this time the hand found no wall. For him, too, the barrier was gone.

"Once through, you are free," he added wonderingly. "Maybe they never foresaw any escapes." He struggled up, sitting with his hands hanging loosely between his knees.

Vye turned his head, looked down the trail. The length of distance lying between them and the safari camp now faced them with a new problem. Neither of them could make that trek on foot.

"We're out, but we aren't back—yet," Hume echoed his thought.

"I was wondering, if *this* door is open—" Vye began.

"The flitter!" Again Hume's mind matched his. "Yes, if those globes aren't hanging around just waiting for us to try."

"They might act only to get us here, not to keep us once we're in." That might be wishful thinking, they wouldn't know until they tried to prove it.

"Give me a hand." Hume held out his own, let Vye pull him to his feet. Weak as he was, he was clear-eyed, plainly clear-headed once more. "Let's go!"

Together they went back through the gap, then tested the absence of the barrier once more, to make sure. Hume laughed. "At least the front door remains open, even if we find the back one closed."

Vye left him sitting by that entrance while he made a quick trip to the cave to pick up the small pack of supplies left them. When he returned they crammed tablets into their mouths, drank feverishly of the lake water, and, with the stimulation of the new energy, set off along the cliff face.

"This wall in the lake," Hume asked suddenly, "you are sure it is artificial?"

"Runs too straight to be anything else, and those projections are evenly spaced. I don't see how it could be natural."

"We'll have to be sure."

Vye thought of that attacking water creature. "No diving in there," he protested. Hume smiled, a stretch of skin far too tight over his jaw now.

"Not us, at least not us now," he agreed. "But the Guild will send another survey."

"What could be the reason for all this?" Vye helped his companion over the loose debris of a cliff slide.

"Information."

"What?"

"Someone—or something—picked our brains while we were out of our heads. Or—" Hume paused suddenly, looked directly at Vye. "I have a vague feeling that you were able to keep going a lot better than I was. That so?"

"Some of the time," Vye admitted.

"That checks. Part of me knew what was going on, but was helpless while that other thing," his smile of moments earlier was wiped away, there was a chill edge in his voice, "picked over my brains, sorted out what it wanted."

Vye shook his head. "I didn't feel that way. Just thick-headed—as if I were sleep walking and yet awake."

"So it took me over, but didn't go all the way with you. Why? Another question for our list."

"Maybe—maybe Wass' techs fixed it so I couldn't be brain-picked, as you call it," Vye offered.

Hume nodded. "Could be—would well be. Come on." He pressed the pace now.

Vye turned to look down the slope suspiciously. Had Hume another warning of menace out of the wood? He could sight no movement there. And from this distance the lake was a topaz sheet of calm which could hide anything. Hume was already several paces ahead, scrambling as if the valley monsters were again on their track.

"What's the matter?" Vye demanded, as he caught up.

"Night coming." Which was true. Then Hume added, "If we can reach the flitter before sunset, we'll have a chance to fly over the lake down there, to make a taping of it before we go."

The energy of the tablets strengthened them so that by the time they reached the crevice door they were moving with their former agility. For a single second Hume hesitated before that slit, almost as if he feared the test he must make. Then he stepped forward and this time into freedom.

They reached the ledge where the flitter perched just as they had seen it last. How long ago that had been they could not have told, but they suspected that days of haze hung in between. Vye searched the sky. No globes winking there— just the flyer alone.

He took his old seat behind the pilot, watched Hume test the relays and responses in the quick run down of a man who has done this chore many times before. But the other gave a little sigh of relief when he finished.

"She's all right, we can lift."

Again they both looked aloft, half fearing to see those malignant herders wink into being to forbid flight. But the sky was as serenely clear of even a drifting cloud as they could hope. Hume pressed a button and they arose vertically with an even progress totally unlike the leap which had taken them out of Wass' camp.

Well above the cliff wall they hovered, and were able to see below the round bowl of the valley prison. Hume touched controls, the flitter descended slowly just above the center of the lake. And from this position they were able to sight the other peculiarity of that body of water, that it was perfectly oval in shape, far too perfect to be an undeveloped product of nature. Hume took a round disk from his equipment belt, fitted it carefully into a slot on the control board and pressed the button below. Then he sent the flitter in a weaving zigzag course well above the surface of the water, so that eventually the flyer passed over every foot of its surface.

And from above, in spite of the turgid quality of the liquid, they could see what did rest on the bottom of that oval. The wall with its sharp corner which Vye had noted from shore level was only part of a water covered erection. It made a design when seen from overhead, a six-pointed star surrounding an oval and in the midst of that oval a black blot which they could not identify.

Hume brought the flitter over in one last sweep. "That's it. We have a full taping."

"What do you think it is?"

"A device set there by an intelligent being, and set a long time ago. This valley wasn't arranged over night, six months ago—or even a year ago. We'll have to let the experts tell us when and for what reason. Now, let's head for home!"

He brought the flitter up and over the valley wall, flying southwest so that they passed over the gap which was the main entrance to the trap. And now he tried the com unit, endeavoring to pick up a signal on which they could beam in for a safe ride.

"That's odd." Under Hume's control the direction finder passed back and forth without bringing any answering code click from the mike. "We may be too far in the mountains to pick up the beam. I wonder . . . " He swept the needle in another direction, slightly to the left.

A crackle spat from the mike. Vye could not read code but the very fury and intensity of that sound suggested panic —even terror.

"What's that?"

Hume spoke without looking away from the control board. "Alarm."

"From the safari?"

"No. Wass." For a long second Hume sat very still, his fingers quiet. The flitter was on the automatic course, taking them out of the mountains, and Vye thought that their air speed was such they were already well removed from that sinister valley.

Hume made a slight adjustment to a dial, and the flitter

banked, coming around on another course. Once more he spun the finder of the com. This time he was answered with a series of well-spaced clicks which lacked the urgency of that other call. Hume listened until the code rattled into silence again.

"They're all right at the safari camp."

"But Wass is in trouble. So what does that matter?" Vye wanted to know.

"It matters this much." Hume spoke slowly as if he must convince himself as well as Vye. "I'm the Guild man on Jumala, and the Guild man is responsible for all civs."

"You can't call him your client!"

Hume shook his head. "No, he's no client. But he's human."

It narrowed down to that when a man was on the frontier worlds—humans stood together. Vye wanted to deny it, but his own emotions, as well as the centuries of age-old tradition, argued him down. Wass was a Veep, one of the criminal parasites dabbling in human misery along more than one solar lane. But he was also human and, as one of their own species, had his claim on them.

Vye watched Hume take over the controls, felt the flitter answer another change of course, then heard the frantic yammer of the distress call as they leveled off to ride its beam in to the hidden camp.

"Automatic." Hume had turned down the volume of the receiver so that the clicks in the mike no longer were so strident. "Set on maximum and left that way."

"They had a force barrier around the camp and they knew about the globes and the watchers." Vye tried to imagine what had happened in that woods clearing.

"The barrier might have shorted. And without the flitter they would have been pinned."

"Could have taken off in the spacer."

"Wass doesn't have the reputation of letting any project get out of his hands."

Vye remembered. "Oh—your billion credit deal."

To his surprise Hume laughed. "Seems all very far and out of orbit now, doesn't it, Lansor? Yes, our billion credit deal—but that was thought out before we knew there were more players around the table than we counted. I wonder . . ."

But what he wondered he did not put into words and a

moment later he added over his shoulder, "Better try to get some rest, boy. We've some time to a set-down."

Vye did sleep, deeply, dreamlessly. And he roused after a gentle shaking to see a beam of light in the sky ahead, though around them was the solid darkness of night.

"That's a warning," Hume explained. "And I can't raise any reply from the camp except a repeat of the distress call. If there is anyone there now, he can't or won't answer."

Against that column of light they could make out the sky-pointed taper of the spacer and the auto-pilot landed them beside that ship in the middle of an area well lighted by the steady shaft of light from the tripod standing where the atom lamp had been on the night they had made their escape from camp.

Climbing stiffly from the small flyer they advanced with caution. A very few minutes later Hume slid his ray tube back into its belt loop.

"Unless they've holed up in the spacer—and I can't see why they'd do that—this camp's deserted. And they haven't taken any equipment with them except maybe a few items they could back-pack."

The ship proved as empty of life as the campsite. A wall seat pulled out too hastily so that it was jammed awry, the com cabin suggested that the leave-taking, when and for what reason, had been a matter of some emergency. Hume did not touch the tape set to keep on broadcasting the call for assistance.

"What now?" Vye wanted to know as they completed the search.

"The safari camp first—and a call for the Patrol."

"Look here," Vye set down the ration container he had found, was emptying it with vast satisfaction of one who had been too long on tablets, "if you beam the Patrol you'll have to talk, won't you?"

Hume went on fitting new charges into his ray tube. "The Patrol has to have a full report. There's no way of bypassing that. Yes, we'll have to give all the story. You needn't worry." He snapped closed the load chamber. "I can clear you all the way. You're the victim, remember."

"I wasn't thinking about that."

"Boy." Hume tossed the tube up in the air, caught it in

his plasta-hand. "I went into this deal with my eyes wide open—why doesn't matter very much now. In fact," he stared beyond Vye out into the empty, lighted camp, "I've begun to wonder about a lot of things—maybe too late. No—we'll call the Patrol and we'll do it not because it is Wass and his men out there, but because we're human and they're human, and there's a nasty set-up here which has already sucked in other humans for its own purposes."

The skeleton in the valley! And how very close they had been themselves to joining that unknown in his permanent residence.

"So now we make time—back to the safari camp. Get our message off to the Patrol and then we'll try to trace Wass and see what we can do. Jumala is off a regular route. The Patrol won't be here tomorrow at sunrise, no matter how much we wish a scouter would planet then."

Vye was quiet as he stowed in the flitter again. As Hume had said, events moved fast. A little while ago he had wanted to settle with this Out-Hunter, wring out of him not only an explanation for his being here, but claim satisfaction for the humiliation of being moved about to suit some others' purposes. Now he was willing to defeat Wass, bring in the Patrol, go up against whatever hid in that lake up there, providing Hume was not the loser. He tried to think why that was so and could not, he only knew it was the truth.

They were both silent as they took off from Wass' deserted camp, sped away over the black blot of the woodland towards the safari headquarters on the plains. There were stars above again but no globes. Just as they had won their freedom from the valley, so they moved without escort on the plains.

But the lights were there—not impinging on the flitter, or patrolling along its line of flight. No, they hung in a glowing cluster ahead when in the dawn the flitter shot away from the woods, headed for the landmark of the safari camp. A crown of lights circled over the camp site, as if those below were in a state of siege.

Hume aimed straight for them and this time the bobbing circle split wide open, broke to left and right. Vye looked below. Though the grayness of the morning was still hardly more than dusk he could not miss those humps spaced at intervals on the land, just beyond the unseen line of the force barrier. The lights above, the beasts below, the safari camp was under guard.

12

"THERE IS only one way they could be moving—toward the mountains." Hume stood in the open space among the bubble tents, facing him the four men of the camp, the three civs and Rovald. "You say it's been seven days, planet time, since I left here. They may have been five days on that trail. If possible we have to stop them before they reach that valley."

"A fantastic story." Chambriss wore the affronted expression of a man who expected no interference with his own concerns. Then catching Hume's eye he added, "Not that we doubt you, Hunter. We have the evidence in those dumb brutes waiting out there. However, by your own story, this Wass is an outside-the-law Veep, on this planet secretly for criminal purposes. Surely there is no reason for us to risk our safety in his behalf. Are you certain he is in any danger at all? You and this young man here have, by your testimony, been into the enemies' territory and have been able to get out again."

"Through a series of fortunate chances which might never occur again." Hume was patient, too patient, Rovald seemed to think. His hand moved, he was holding a ray tube so that a simple movement of the wrist could send a crisping blast across all the rest of the party.

"I say, stop this yapping and get out there and pick up the Veep!"

"I intend to—after I call the Patrol."

Rovald's tube was now aimed directly at Hume. "No Patrol!" he ordered.

82

"This wrangling has gone far enough." It was Yactisi who spoke with an authority which startled them all. And as their attention swung to him, he was already in action.

Rovald cried out, the weapon spun from his fingers, fingers which were slowly reddening. Yactisi nodded with satisfaction and he held his electo pole ready for a second attack. Vye scooped up the tube which had whirled across the ground to strike against his borrowed boot.

"I'll set the call for the Patrol, then I'll try to locate Wass," Hume stated.

"Sensible procedure," Yactisi approved in his dry voice. "You believe that you are now immune to whatever force this alien installation controls?"

"It would seem so."

"Then, of course, you must go."

"Why?" Chambriss countered for the second time. "Suppose he isn't so immune after all? Suppose he gets out there and is captured again? He's our pilot—do you want to be planet bound *here*?

"This man is also a pilot." Starns indicated Rovald, who was nursing his numb hand.

"Since he, too, is one of these criminals, he's not to be trusted!" Chambriss shot back. "Hunter, I demand that you take us off planet at once! And it is only fair to inform you that I also intend to prefer charges against you and against the Guild. Empty world! Just how empty have we found this world?"

"But, Gentlehomo," Starns showed no signs of any emotion but eager curiosity, "to be here at this time is a privilege we could not hope to equal except by good fortune! The T-Casts will be avid for our stories."

What had that to do with the matter, puzzled Vye. But he saw Starns' reminder produce a quick change in Chambriss.

"The T-Casts," he repeated, his expression of anger smoothing away. "Yes, of course, this is, in a manner of speaking, a truly historic occasion. We are in a unique position!"

Had Yactisi smiled? That change of lip line had been so slight Vye could not call it a smile. But Starns appeared to have found the right way to handle Chambriss. And it was the same little man who offered his services in another way when he said, diffidently to Hume:

"I have some experience with coms, Hunter. Do you wish me to send your message and take over the unit until you return? I gather," he added with a certain delicacy, "that it will not be expedient for your gearman to engage in that duty now."

So it was that Starns was installed in the com cabin of the spacer, sending out the request for Patrol aid, while Rovald was locked in the storage compartment of the same ship, pending arrival of those same authorities. As Hume sorted out supplies and Vye loaded them into the waiting flitter, Yactisi approached the Hunter.

"You have a definite plan of search?"

"Just to cast north from their camp. If they've been gone long enough to hit the foothills we may be able to sight them climbing. Otherwise, we'll go all the way up to the valley, wait for them there."

"You don't believe that they will be released after they have been—processed?"

Hume shook his head. "I don't think we would have been free, Gentlehomo, if it hadn't been for a series of fortunate accidents."

"Yes, though you didn't give us many details about that, Hunter."

Hume put down the needler he had been charging. He studied Yactisi across that weapon.

"Who are you?" His voice was soft but carried a snap.

For the first time Vye saw the tall, lean civ really smile.

"A man of many interests, Hunter—shall we let it go at that for the present? Though I assure you that Wass is not one of them in the way you might believe."

Gray eyes met brown, held so straightly. Then Hume spoke. "I believe you. But I have told you the truth."

"I have never doubted that—only the amount of it. There must be more talking later on—you understand that?"

"I never thought otherwise." Hume set the needler inside the flitter. The civ smiled again, this time including Vye in that evidence of good will before he walked away.

Hume made no comment. "That does it," he told his companion. "Still want to go?"

"If you do—and you can't do it alone." No man could take on the valley and Wass and his men.

Hume made no comment. They had rested briefly after

their return to the safari camp, and Vye had been supplied with clothing from Hume's bags, so that now he wore the uniform of the Guild. He went armed, too, with the equipment belt taken from Rovald and that other's weapons, needler and tube. At least they started on their dubious rescue mission with every aid the safari camp could muster.

It was mid-afternoon when the flitter took to the air once again, scattering the hovering globes. There was no alteration in the ranks of the blue watchers waiting—for the barrier to go down, or someone in the camp to step beyond that protection?

"They're stupid," Vye said.

"Not stupid, just geared to one set of actions," Hume returned.

"Which could mean that what sends them here can't change its orders."

"Good guess. I'd say that they were governed by something akin to our tapes. No provision made for any innovations."

"So the guiding intelligence could be long gone."

"I think it has been." Hume then changed the subject sharply.

"How did you get into service at the Starfall?"

It was hard now to think back to Nahuatl—as if the Vye Lansor who had been swamper in that den of the port town was a different person altogether. In that patch of memories into which Rynch Brodie still intruded he hunted for the proper answer.

"I cculdn't hold the state jobs. And once you get the habit of eating, you don't starve willingly."

"Why not the state jobs?"

"Without premium they're all low-rung tenders' places. I tried hard enough. But to sit pressing buttons when a light flashed, hour after hour—" Vye shook his head. "They said I was too erratic and gave me the shove. One more move on and it would have been compulsive conditioning. I turned port-drift instead."

"Ever thought of trying for a loan premium?"

Vye laughed shortly. "Loan premium? That's a true fantasy if you've been job hopping. None of the companies will take a chance on a man with an in and out record. Oh, I tried . . . " That memory arose to the surface, clear and very chilling. Yes, he had tried to break out of the net the law and custom had put around him from the day he had been made a state child. "No—it was conditioning, or port-drift."

"And you chose port-drift?"

"I was still me—as long as I stayed away from conditioning."

"Then you became Rynch Brodie in spite of your flight."

"No—well, maybe, for a while. But I'm still Vye Lansor here."

"Yes, here. And I don't think you'll have to worry about raising a premium to get a new start. You can claim victim compensation, you know."

Vye was silent, but Hume did not let him remain so.

"When the Patrol arrives, you put in your claim. I'll back you."

"You can't."

"That's where you're mistaken," Hume told him crisply. "I've already taped a full story back at the spacer—it's on record now."

Vye frowned. The Hunter seemed determined to ask for the worst the Patrol—or the planet police back on Nahuatl—could deal out. A case of illegal conditioning was about as serious as you could get.

They shot along the diagonal of the triangle made by three points, the mountain valley, Wass' camp, and the safari headquarters, heading to the slopes up which the men must be herded if the beasts were shepherding them to the mountain valley. Vye, surveying the forest thick below, began to doubt they would ever be able to pick them up before they reached the valley gate.

Hume took a weaving course, zigzagging back and forth, while they both watched intently for a glint from one of the globes, any movement which would betray that trail. And it was on one of the upper slopes that the flitter passed over two of the blue beasts lumbering along. Neither of the creatures paid any attention to the flyer, they moved with purpose on some mission of their own.

"Maybe the tail end of the hunting pack," Hume commented.

He sent the flyer hovering over a stunted line of trees and brush. Beyond that was bare rock. But though they hung for moments, nothing moved into that open.

"Wrong scent somehow." Hume brought the flitter around.

He had it on manual control now, keeping it answering to the quick changes of his will.

A longer sweep supplied the answer—a vegetation roofed slit running back into the uplands, in a way resembling the crevice through which they had originally found their way into this country. Hume brought the flyer along that. But if the men they sought were pushing their way through below they could not be sighted from the air. At last, with evening drawing in, Hume was forced to admit failure.

"Wait by the gap?" Vye asked.

"Have to now." Hume glanced about. "I'd say maybe tomorrow—mid-morning before they make it that far—*if* they are here. We'll have plenty of time."

Time for what? To make ready for a pitched battle with Wass—or with the beasts herding him? To try in the space of hours to solve the mystery of the lake?

"Do you think we could blast that thing in the lake?" Vye asked.

"We might be able to, just might. But that must be the last resort. We want that in working order for the X-Tee men to study. No, we'd better plan to hold Wass at the gate, wait for the Patrol to come in."

Less than an hour later after a soaring approach, Hume brought the flitter down with neat skill on the top of one of the cliffs which helped to form the portal of the gap. There was no difference in the scene below, save that where the two bodies of the blue beasts had lain there were now only clean and shining bones.

Darkness spread out from the lake woods like a growing stain of evil promise as the sun fell behind the peaks. Night came earlier here than in the plains.

"Watch!" Vye had been gazing down the gap; he was the first to note that movement in the cloaking bush.

Out of the cover trotted a four-footed, antlered animal he had not seen before.

"Syken deer," Hume identified. "But why in the mountains? It's a long way from its home range."

The deer did not pause, but headed directly for the gap and, as it neared, Vye saw that its brown coat was roughed with patches of white froth, while more dripped from the pale pink tongue protruding from its open jaws, and its shrunken sides heaved.

"Driven!" Hume picked up a stone, hurled it to strike the ground ahead of the deer.

The creature did not start, nor show any sign of seeing the rock fall. It trotted on at the same wearied pace, passed the portal rocks into the valley. Then it stood still, wedge-shaped head up, black horns displayed, while the nose flaps expanded, testing the air, until it bounded toward the lake, disappearing in the woods.

Though they shared watches during the night there were no other signs of life, nor did the deer reappear from the woods. With the mid-morning there was a sudden sound to warn them—a wild cry which must have come from a human throat. Hume tossed one of the needlers to Vye, took the other, and they scrambled down to the floor of the gap passage.

Wass did not lead his men, he came behind the reeling trio as if he had joined the blasts as driver. And while his men wavered, staggered, gave the appearance of nearly complete exhaustion, he still walked with a steady tread, in command of his wits, his fears, and the company.

As the first of the men blundered on, a fresh trickle of red running down his bruised face, Hume called:

"Wass!"

The Veep stopped short. He made no move to unsling the needler he carried, its barrel pointing skyward over his shoulder, but his round head with its upstanding comb of hair swung slightly from side to side.

"Stop—Wass—this is a trap!"

His three men kept on. Vye moved, for Peake leading that wavering group, stumbled, would have fallen had not the younger man advanced from the shadows to steady him.

"Vye!" Hume made his name a warning.

He had only time to glance around. Wass, his broad face impassive except for the eyes—those burning madman's eyes—was aiming a ray tube.

Broken free of his hold, Peake fell to the right, came up against Hume. As Vye went down he saw Wass dart forward at a speed he wouldn't have believed a driven man could summon. The Veep lunged, escaping the shot the Hunter had no time to aim, rolled, and came up with the needler Vye had dropped.

Then Hume, hampered by Peake's feeble clawing, met

head on the swinging barrel of that weapon. He gave a startled grunt and smashed back against the cliff, a wave of scarlet blood streaming down the side of his head.

The momentum of Wass' charge carried him on. He collided with his men, and the last thing Vye saw, was the huddle of all four of them, flailing arms and legs, spinning on through the gate into the valley with Wass' hoarse, wordless shouting, bringing echoes from the cliffs.

13

HE LAY against a rock, and it was quiet again, except for a small whimpering sound which hurt, joined with the eating pain in his side. Vye turned his head, smelled burned cloth and flesh. Cautiously he tried to move, bring his hand across his body to the belt at his waist. One small part of his mind was very clear—if he could get his fingers to the packet there, and the contents of that packet to his mouth, the pain would go away, and maybe he could slip back into the darkness again.

Somehow he did it, pulled the packet out of its container pouch, worked the fingers of his one usable hand until he shredded open the end of the covering. The tablets inside, spilled out. But he had three or four of them in his grasp. Laboriously he brought his hand up, mouthed them all together, chewing their bitterness, swallowing them as best he could without water.

Water—the lake! For a moment he was back in time, feeling for the water bulbs he should be carrying. Then the incautious movement of his questing fingers brought a sudden stab of raw, red agony and he moaned.

The tablets worked. But he did not slide back into unconsciousness again as the throbbing torture became something remote and untroubling. With his good arm he braced himself against the cliff, managed to sit up.

Sun flashed on the metal barrel of a needler which lay in the trampled dust between him and another figure, still very still, with a pool of blood about the head. Vye waited for a steadying breath or two, then started the infinitely long journey of several feet which separated him from Hume.

He was panting heavily when he crawled close enough to touch the Hunter. Hume's face, cheek down in the now sodden dust, was dabbled with congealing blood. As Vye turned the hunter's head, it rolled limply. The other side was a mass of blood and dust, too thick to afford Vye any idea of how serious a hurt Hume had taken. But he was still alive.

With his good hand Vye thrust his numb and useless left one into the front of his belt. Then, awkwardly he tried to tend Hume. After a close inspection he thought that the mass of blood had come from a ragged tear in the scalp above the temple and the bone beneath had escaped damage. From Hume's own first-aid pack he crushed tablets into the other's slack mouth, hoping they would dissolve if the Hunter could not swallow. Then he relaxed against the cliff to wait—for what he could not have said.

Wass' party had gone on into the valley. When Vye turned his head to look down the slope he could see nothing of them. They must have tried to push on to the lake. The flitter was at the top of the cliff, as far out of his reach now as if it were in planetary orbit. There was only the hope that a rescue party from the safari camp might come. Hume had set the directional beam on the flyer, when he had brought her down, to serve as a beacon for the Patrol, if and when Starns was lucky enough to contact a cruiser.

"Hmmm . . ." Hume's mouth moved, cracked the drying bloody mask on his lips and chin. His eyes blinked open and he lay staring up at the sky.

"Hume—" Vye was startled at the sound of his own voice, so thready and weak, and by the fact that he found it difficult to speak at all.

The other's head turned; now the eyes were on him and there was a spark of awareness in them.

"Wass?" The whisper was as strained as his own had been.

"In there." Vye's hand lifted from Hume's chest indicating the valley.

"Not good." Hume blinked again. "How bad?" His attention was not for his own hurt; his eyes searched Vye. And the latter glanced down at his side.

By some chance, perhaps because of his struggle with Peake, Wass' beam had not struck true, the main core of the bolt passing between his arm and his side, burning both. How deeply he could not tell, in fact he did not want to find out. It was enough that the tablets had banished the pain now.

"Seared a little," he said. "You've a bad cut on your head."

Hume frowned. "Can we make the flitter?"

Vye moved, then relaxed quickly into his former position. "Not now," he evaded, knowing that neither of them would be able to take that climb.

"Beam on?" Hume repeated Vye's thoughts of moments before. "Patrol coming?"

Yes, eventually the Patrol would come—but when? Hours —days? Time was their enemy now. He did not have to say any of that, they both knew.

"Needler—" Hume's head had turned in the other direction; now his hand pointed waveringly to the weapon in the dust.

"They won't be back," Vye stated the obvious. Those others had been caught in the trap, the odds on their return without aid were very high.

"Needler!" Hume repeated more firmly, and tried to sit up, falling back with a sharp intake of breath.

Vye edged around, stretched out his leg and scraped the toe of his boot into the loop of the carrying sling, drawing the weapon up to where he could get his hand on it. As he steadied it across his knee Hume spoke again:

"Watch for trouble!"

"They all went in," Vye protested.

But Hume's eyes had closed again. "Trouble—maybe . . ." His voice trailed off. Vye rested his hand on the stock of the needler.

"Hooooool!"

That beast wail—as they had heard it in the valley! Somewhere from the wood. Vye brought the needler around, so that the sights pointed in that direction. There death might be hunting, but there was nothing he could do.

A scream, filled with all the agony of a man in torment,

caught up on the echoes of that other cry. Vye sighted a wild waving of bushes. A figure, very small and far away, crawled into the open on hands and knees and then crumpled into only a shadowy blot on the moss. Again the beast's cry, and a shouting!

Vye watched a second man back out of the trees, still facing whatever pursued him. He caught the glint of sun on what must be a ray tube. Leaves crisped into a black hole, curls of smoke arose along the path of that blast.

The man kept on backing, passed the inert body of his companion, glancing now and then over his shoulder at the slope up which he was making a slow but steady way. He no longer rayed the bush, but there was the crackle of a small fire outlining the ragged hole his beam had cut.

Back two strides, three. Then he turned, made a quick dash, again facing around after he had gained some yards in the open. Vye saw now it was Wass.

Another dash and an about face. But this time to confront the enemy. There were three of them, as monstrous as those Vye and Hume had fought in the same place. And one of them was wounded, swinging a charred forepaw before it, and giving voice to a wild frenzy of roars.

Wass leveled the ray tube, centered sights on the beast nearest to him. The man hammered at the firing button with the flat of his other hand, and almost paid for that second of distraction with his life, for the creature made one of those lightning swift dashes Vye had so luckily escaped. The clawed forepaw tore a strip from the shoulder of Wass' tunic, left sprouting red furrows behind. But the man had thrown the useless tube into its face, was now running for the gap.

Vye held the needler braced against his knee to fire. He saw the dart quiver in the upper arm of the beast, and it halted to pull out that sliver of dangerously poisoned metal, crumpled it into a tight twist. Vye continued to fire, never sure of his aim, but seeing those slivers go home in thick legs, in outstretched forelimbs, in wide, pendulous bellies. Then there were three blue shapes lying on the slope behind the man running straight for the gap.

Wass hit the invisible barrier full force, was hurled back, to lie gasping on the turf, but already raising himself to crawl again to the gateway he saw and could not believe was barred. Vye closed his eyes. He was very tired now—tired and sleepy—maybe the pain pills were bringing the secondary form of relief. But he could hear, just beyond, the man who beat at that unseen curtain, first in anger and fear, and then just in fear, until the fear was a lonesome crying that went on and on until even that last feeble assault on the barrier failed.

"We have here the tape report of Ras Hume, Out-Hunter of the Guild."

Vye watched the officer in the black and silver of the Patrol, a black and silver modified with the small, green, eye badge of X-Tee, with level and hostile gaze.

"Then you know the story." He was going to make no additions nor explanations. Maybe Hume had cleared him. All right, that was all he would ask, to be free to go his way and forget about Jumala—and Ras Hume.

He had not seen the Hunter since they had both been loaded into the Patrol flitter in the gap. Wass had come out of the valley a witless, dazed creature, still under the mental influence of whoever, or whatever, had set that trap. As far as Vye knew the Veep had not yet recovered his full senses, he might never do so. And if Hume had not dictated that confession to damn himself before the Patrol, he might have escaped. They could suspect—but they would have had no proof.

"You continue to refuse to tape?" The officer favored him with one of the closed-jaw looks Vye had often seen on the face of authority.

"I have my rights."

"You have the right to claim victim compensation—a good compensation, Lansor."

Vye shrugged and then winced at a warning from the tender skin over ribs.

"I make no claim, and no tape," he repeated. And he intended to go on saying that as long as they asked him. This was the second visit in two days and he was getting a little tired of it all. Perhaps he should do as prudence dictated and demand to be returned to Nahuatl. Only his odd, unexplainable desire to at least see Hume kept him from making the request they would have to honor.

"You had better reconsider." Authority resumed.

"Rights of person—" Vye almost grinned as he recited that. For the first time in his pushed-around life he could use that particular phrase and make it stick. He thought there was a sour twist to the officer's mouth, but the other still retained his impersonal tone as he spoke into the intership com:

"He refused to make a tape."

Vye waited for the other's next move. This should mark the end of their interview. But instead the officer appeared to relax the restraint of his official manner. He brought a viv-root case from an inner pocket, offered a choice of contents to Vye, who gave an instant and suspicious refusal by shake of head. The officer selected one of the small tubes, snapped off the protecto-nib, and set it between his lips for a satisfying and lengthy pull. Then the panel of the cabin door pushed open, and Vye sat up with a jerk as Ras Hume, his head banded with a skin-core covering, entered.

The officer waved his hand at Vye with the air of one turning over a problem. "You were entirely right. And he's all yours, Hume."

Vye looked from one to the other. With Hume's tape in official hands why wasn't the Hunter under restraint? Unless, because they were aboard the Patrol cruiser, the officers didn't think a closer confinement was necessary. Yet the Hunter wasn't acting the role of prisoner very well. In fact he perched on a wall-flip seat with the ease of one completely at home, accepted the viv-root Vye had refused.

"So you won't make a tape," he asked cheerfully.

"You act as if you want me to!" Vye was so completely baffled by this odd turn of action that his voice came out almost plaintively.

"Seeing as how a great deal of time and effort went into placing you in the position where you *could* give us that tape, I must admit some disappointment."

"Give *us?*" Vye echoed.

The officer removed the viv-root from between his lips. "Tell him the whole sad story, Hume."

But Vye began to guess. Life in the Starfall, or as portdrift, either sharpened the wits or deadened them. Vye's had suffered the burnishing process. "A set-up?"

"A set-up," Hume agreed. Then he glanced at the Patrol officer a little defensively. "I might as well tell the whole truth—this didn't quite begin on the right side of the law. I had my reasons for wanting to make trouble for the Kogan estate, only not because of the credits involved." He moved his plasta-flesh hand. "When I found that L-B from the Largo Drift and saw the possibilities, did a little day dreaming—I worked out this scheme. But I'm a Guild man and as it happens, I want to stay one. So I reported to one of the Masters and told him the whole story—why I hadn't taped on the records my discovery on Jumala.

"When he passed along the news of the L-B to the Patrol, he also suggested that there might be room for fraud along the way I had thought it out. That started a chain reaction. It happened that the Patrol wanted Wass. But he was too big and slick to be caught in a case which couldn't be broken in court. They thought that here was just the bait he might snap at, and I was the one to offer it to him. He could check on me, learn that I had excellent reason to do what I said I was doing. So I went to him with my story and he liked it. We made the plan work just as I had outlined it. And he planted Rovald on me as a check. But I didn't know Yactisi was a plant, also."

The Patrol officer smiled. "Insurance," he waved the vivroot, "just insurance."

"What we didn't foresee was this complicating alien trouble. You were to be collected as the castaway, brought back to the Center and then, once Wass was firmly enmeshed, the Patrol would blow the thing wide open. Now we do have Wass, with your tape we'll have him for good, subject to complete reconditioning. But we also have an X-Tee puzzle which will keep the services busy for some time. And we would like your tape."

Vye watched Hume narrowly. "Then you're an agent?"

Hume shook his head. "No, just what I said I am, an Out-Hunter who happened to come into some knowledge that will assist in straightening out a few crooked quirks in several systems. I have no love for the Kogan clan, but to help bring down a Veep of Wass' measure does aid in reinstating one's self-esteem."

"This victim compensation—I *could* claim it, even though the deal was a set-up?"

"You'll have first call on Wass' assets. He has plenty invested in legitimate enterprises, though we'll probably never locate all his hidden funds. But everything we can get open title to will be impounded. Have something to do with your share?" inquired the officer.

"Yes."

Hume was smiling subtly. He was a different man from the one Vye had known on Jumala. "Premium for the Guild is one thousand credits down, two thousand for training and say another for about the best field outfit you can buy. That'll give you maybe another two or three thousand to save for your honorable retirement."

"How did you know?" Vye began and then had to laugh in spite of himself as Hume replied:

"I didn't. Good guess, eh? Well, zoom out your recorder, Commander. I think you are going to have some very free speech now." He got to his feet. "You know, the Guild has a stake in this alien discovery. We may just find that we haven't seen the last of that valley after all, recruit."

He was gone and Vye, eager to have the past done with, and the future beginning, reached for the dictation mike.

VOODOO PLANET

1

TALK OF HEAT—or better not—on Xecho. This water-logged world combined all the most unattractive features of a steam bath and one could only dream of coolness, greenness—more land than a stingy string of islands.

The young man on the promontory above the crash of the waves wore the winged cap of a spaceman with the insignia of a cargo-master and not much else, save a pair of very short shorts. He wiped one hand absently across his bare chest and brought it away damp as he studied, through protective sun goggles, the treacherous promise of the bright sea. One *could* swim—if he wanted to lose most of his skin. There were minute organisms in that liquid that smacked their lips—if they had lips—every time they thought of a Terran.

Dane Thorson licked his own lips, tasting salt, and plodded back through the sand of the spaceport to the berth of the *Solar Queen*. This had been a long day, and one with more snarl-ups than he cared to count, keeping him on a constant, dogged trot between the ship and the fitting yard where riggers labored with the slowest motions possible to the human body—or so it seemed to the exasperated acting-cargo-master of the Free Trader. Captain Jellico had long ago taken refuge in his cabin to preserve the remnants of his temper. Dane had been allowed no such escape.

The *Queen* had a schedule for refitting to serve as a mail ship, and that time allowance did not allow for humidity playing the devil with the innards of robot fitters. She *had* to be ready to lift when the Combine ship now plying that run set down and formally signed off in her favor. Luckily, most of the work was done and Dane had given a last searching inspection before signing the rigger's book and reporting to his captain.

The air-conditioned interior of the *Queen* comforted him as he climbed to his quarters. Ship air was flat, chemically pure but unappetizing stuff. Today it was a relief to breathe. Dane went on to the bather. At least there was no lack of water—with the local skinners filtered out. It was chill but relaxing on his gaunt young body.

He was sealing on his lightest tunic when the ramp buzzer sounded. A visitor—oh, not the supervisor-rigger again! Dane went to answer with dragging feet. For the crew of the *Queen* at the moment numbered exactly four, with himself for general errand boy. Captain Jellico was in his quarters two levels above, Medic Tau was presumably overhauling his supplies, and Sindbad, ship's cat, asleep in some empty cabin.

Dane jerked his tunic into place, very much on his guard as he came to the head of the ramp. But it was not the supervisor-rigger. Dane, thoroughly used to unusual-appearing strangers, both human and alien, was impressed by this visitor.

He was tall, this quiet man, his great height accented by a fit leanness, a narrowness of waist and hip, a length of leg and arm. His main article of clothing was the universal shorts of the Xecho settler. But, being fashioned of saffron yellow, they were the more brilliant because of his darkness of skin. For he was not the warm brown of the Terran Negroes Dane had served beside, though he shared their general features. His flesh was really black, black with an almost bluish sheen. Instead of shirt or tunic, his deep chest was crossed by two wide straps, the big medallion marking their intersection giving forth flashes of gem fire when he breathed. He wore at his belt not the standard stun gun of a spaceman, but a weapon which resembled the more deadly Patrol blaster, as well as a long knife housed in a jeweled and fringed sheath. To the eye he was an example of barbaric force tamed and trimmed to civilized efficiency.

He saluted, palm out, and spoke Galactic Basic with only a suggestion of accent.

"I am Kort Asaki. I believe Captain Jellico expects me."

"Yes, sir!" Dane snapped to attention. So this was the Chief Ranger from fabulous Khatka, Xecho's sister planet.

The other ascended the cat ladder easily, missing no detail of the ship's interior as he passed. His expression was still one of polite interest as his guide rapped on the panel door of Jellico's cabin. And a horrible screech from Queex, the captain's pet hoobat, drowned out any immediate answer. Then followed that automatic thump on the floor of the blue-feathered, crab-parrot-toad's cage, announcing that its master was in residence.

Since the captain's cordial welcome extended only to his guest, Dane regretfully descended to the mess cabin to make unskilled preparations for supper—though there was not much you could do to foul up concentrates in an automatic cooker.

"Company?" Tau sat beyond the cooking unit nursing a mug of Terran coffee. "And do you *have* to serve music with the meals, especially that particular selection?"

Dane flushed, stopped whistling in mid-note. "Terran Bound" *was* old and pretty well worn out; he didn't know why he always unconsciously sounded off with that.

"A Chief Ranger from Khatka just came on board," he reported, carefully offhand, as he busied himself reading labels. He knew better than to serve fish or any of its derivatives in disguise again.

"Khatka!" Tau sat up straighter. "Now there's a planet worth visiting."

"Not on Free Trader's pay," commented Dane.

"You can always hope to make a big strike, boy. But what I wouldn't give to lift ship for there!"

"Why? You're no hunter. How come you want to heat jets for that port?"

"Oh, I don't care about the game preserves, though they're worth seeing too. It's the people themselves—"

"But they're Terran settlers, or at least from Terran stock, aren't they?"

"Sure." Tau sipped his coffee slowly. "But there are settlers and settlers, son. And a lot depends upon when they left Terran and why, and who they were—also what happened to them after they landed out here."

"And Khatkans are really special?"

"Well, they have an amazing history. The colony was founded by escaped prisoners—and just one racial stock. They took off from Earth close to the end of the Second Atomic War. That was a race war, remember? Which made it doubly ugly." Tau's mouth twisted in disgust. "As if the color of a man's skin makes any difference in what lies under it! One side in that line-up tried to take over Africa—herded most of the natives into a giant concentration camp and practiced genocide on a grand scale. Then they were cracked themselves, hard and heavy. During the confusion some survivors in the camp staged a revolt, helped by the enemy. They captured an experimental station hidden in the center of the camp and made a break into space in two ships which had been built there. That voyage must have been a nightmare, but they were desperate. Somehow they made it out here to the rim and set down on Khatka without power enough to take off again—and by then most of them were dead.

"But we humans, no matter what our race, are a tough breed. The refugees discovered that climatically their new world was not too different from Africa, a lucky chance which might happen only once in a thousand times. So they thrived, the handful who survived. But the white technicians they had kidnapped to run the ships didn't. For they set up a color bar in reverse. The lighter your skin, the lower you were in the social scale. By that kind of selective breeding the present Khatkans are very dark indeed.

"They reverted to the primitive for survival. Then, about two hundred years ago, long before the first Survey Scout discovered them, something happened. Either the parent race mutated, or, as sometimes occurs, a line of people of superior gifts emerged—not in a few isolated births, but with surprising regularity in five family clans. There was a short period of power struggle until they realized the foolishness of civil war and formed an oligarchy, heading a loose tribal organization. With the Five Families to push and lead, a new civilization developed, and when Survey came to call they were no longer savages. Combine bought the trade rights about seventy-five years ago. Then the Company and the Five Families got together and marketed a luxury item to the galaxy. You know how every super-jet big shot on twenty-five planets wants to say he's hunted on Khatka. And if he can point out a qraz head on his wall, or wear a tail bracelet, he's able to strut with the best. To holiday on Khatka is both fabulous and fashionable—and very, very profitable for the natives and for Combine who sells transportation to the travelers."

"I hear they have poachers, too," Dane remarked.

"Yes, that naturally follows. You know what a glam skin brings on the market. Wherever you have a rigidly controlled export you're going to have poachers and smugglers. But the Patrol doesn't go to Khatka. The natives handle their own criminals. Personally, I'd cheerfully take a ninety-nine-year sentence in the Lunar mines in place of what the Khatkans dish out to a poacher they net!"

"So that rumor has spread satisfactorily!"

Coffee slopped over the brim of Tau's mug and Dane dropped the packet of steak concentrate he was about to feed into the cooker. Chief Ranger Asaki loomed in the doorway of the mess as suddenly as if he had been teleported to that point.

The medic rose to his feet and smiled politely at the visitor.

"Do I detect in that observation, sir, the suggestion that the tales I have heard were deliberately set to blast where they would do the most good as deterrents?"

A fleeting grin broke the impassive somberness of the black face.

"I was informed you are a man skilled in 'magic,' Medic. You certainly display the traditional sorcerer's quickness of wit. But this rumor is also truth." The quirk of good humor had gone again, and there was an edge in the Chief's Ranger's voice which cut. "Poachers on Khatka would welcome the Patrol in place of the attention they now receive."

He came into the mess cabin, Jellico behind him, and Dane pulled down two of the snap seats. He was holding a mug under the spout of the coffee dispenser as the captain made introductions.

"Thorson—our acting-cargo-master."

"Thorson," the Khatkan acknowledged with a grave nod of his head, and then glanced down to floor level with a look of surprise. Weaving a pattern about his legs, purring loudly, Sindbad was offering an unusually fervent welcome of his own. The Ranger went down on one knee, his hand out for Sindbad's inquiring sniff. Then the cat butted that dark palm, batted at it playfully with claw-sheathed paw.

"A Terran cat! It is of the lion family?"

"Far removed," Jellico supplied. "You'd have to add a lot of bulk to Sindbad to promote him to the lion class."

"We have only the old tales." Asaki sounded almost wistful as the cat jumped to his knee and clawed for a hold on his chest belts. "But I do not believe that lions were ever so friendly toward my ancestors."

Dane would have removed the cat, but the Khatkan arose with Sindbad, still purring loudly, resting in the crook of his arm. The Ranger was smiling with a gentleness which changed the whole arrogant cast of his countenance.

"Do not bring this one to Khatka with you, Captain, or you will never take him away again. Those who dwell in the inner courts would not let him vanish from their sight. Ah, so this pleases you, small lion?" He rubbed Sindbad gently under the throat and the cat stretched his neck, his yellow eyes half closed in bliss.

"Thorson"—the Captain turned to Dane—"that arrival report on my desk was the final one from Combine?"

"Yes, sir. There's no hope of the *Rover* setting down here before that date."

Asaki sat down, still holding the cat. "So you see, Captain, fortune has arranged it all. You have two tens of days. Four days to go in my cruiser, four days for your return here, and the rest to explore the preserve. We could not ask for better luck, for I do not know when our paths may cross again. In the normal course of events I will not have another mission to Xecho for a year, perhaps longer. Also—" He hesitated and then spoke to Tau. "Medic, Captain Jellico has informed me that you have made a study of magic on many worlds."

"That is so, sir."

"Do you then believe that it is real force, or that it is only a superstition for child-people who set up demons to howl petitions to when some darkness falls upon them?"

"Some of the magic I have seen is trickery, some of it founded upon an inner knowledge of men and their ways which a shrewd witch doctor can use to his advantage. There always remains"—Tau put down his mug—"there always remains a small residue of happenings and results for which we have not yet found any logical explanations—"

"And I believe," Asaki interrupted, "it is also true that a race can be conditioned from birth to be sensitive to forms of magic so that men of that blood are particularly susceptible." That was more of a statement than a question, but Tau answered it.

"That is very true. A Lamorian, for example, can be 'sung' to death. I have witnessed such a case. But upon a Terran or another off-world man the same suggestion would have no effect."

"Those who settled Khatka brought such magic with them." The Chief Ranger's fingers still moved about Sindbad's jaw and throat soothingly, but his tone was chill, the coldest thing in the cramped space of the mess cabin.

"Yes, a highly developed form of it," Tau agreed.

"More highly developed perhaps than even you can believe, Medic!" That came in a hiss of cold rage. "I think that its present manifestation—death by a beast that is not a beast—could be worth your detailed study."

"Why?" Tau came bluntly to the point.

"Because it is a killing magic and it is being carefully used to rid my world of key men, men we need badly. If there is a weak point in this cloudy attack shaping against us, we must learn it, and soon!"

It was Jellico who added the rest. "We are invited to visit Khatka and survey a new hunting range as Chief Ranger Asaki's personal term guests."

Dane drew a deep breath of wonder. Guest rights on Khatka were jealously guarded—they were too valuable to their owners to waste. Whole families lived on the income from the yearly rental of even half a one. But the Rangers, by right of office, had several which they could grant to visiting scientists or men from other worlds holding positions similar to their own. To have such an opportunity offered to an ordinary Trader was almost incredible.

His wonder was matched by Tau's and must have been plain to read for the Chief Ranger smiled.

"For a long time, Captain Jellico and I have exchanged biological data on alien life-forms—his skill in photographing such, his knowledge as an xenobiologist are widely recognized. And so I have permission for him to visit the new Zoboru preserve, not yet officially opened. And you, Medic Tau, your help or at least your diagnosis, we need in another direction. So, one expert comes openly, another not so openly. Though, Medic, your task is approved by my superiors. And"—he glanced at Dane—"perhaps to muddle the trail for the suspicious, shall we not ask this young man also?"

Dane's eyes went to the captain. Jellico was always fair and his crew would have snapped into action on his word alone—even if they were fronting a rain of Thorkian death darts and that order was to advance. But, on the other hand, Dane would never have asked a favor, and the best he hoped for was to be able to perform his duties without unfavorable comment upon their commission. He had no reason to believe Jellico was willing to agree to this.

"You have two weeks' planet-side leave coming, Thorson. If you want to spend it on Khatka . . ." Jellico actually grinned then. "I take it that you do. When do we up-ship, sir?"

"You said that you must wait for the return of your other crew members—shall we say mid-afternoon tomorrow?" The Chief Ranger stood up and put Sindbad down though the cat protested with several sharp meows.

"Small lion"—the tall Khatkan spoke to the cat as to an equal—"this is your jungle, and mine lies elsewhere. But should you ever grow tired of traveling the stars, there is always a home for you in my courts."

When the Chief Ranger went out the door, Sindbad did not try to follow, but he uttered one mournful little cry of protest and loss.

"So he wants a trouble shooter, does he?" Tau asked. "All right, I'll try to hunt out his goblins for him; it'll be worth that to visit Khatka!"

Dane, remembering the hot glare of the Xecho spaceport, the sea one could not swim in, contrasted that with the tridees he had seen of the green hunters' paradise on the next planet of the system. "Yes, sir!" he echoed and made a haphazard choice for the cooker.

"Don't be too lighthearted," Tau warned. "I'll say that any

stew which was too hot for that Ranger to handle might give us burned fingers—and quick. When we land on Khatka, walk softly and look over your shoulder, and be prepared for the worst."

II

LIGHTNING PLAYED along the black ridges above them and below was a sheer drop to a river which was only a silver thread. Under their boots, man-made and yet dominating the wildness of jungle and mountain, was a platform of rock slabs, fused to support a palace of towering yellow-white walls and curved cups of domes, a palace which was also half fortress, half frontier post.

Dane set his hands on the parapet of the river drop, blinked as a lightning bolt crackled in a sky-splitting glare of violet fire. This was about as far from the steaming islands of Xecho as a man could imagine.

"The demon graz prepare for battle." Asaki nodded toward the distant crackling.

Captain Jellico laughed. "Supposed to be whetting their tusks, eh? I wouldn't care to meet a graz that could produce such a display by mere tusk whetting."

"No? But think of the reward for the tracker who discovers where such go to die. To find the graveyard of the graz herds would make any man wealthy beyond dreams."

"How much truth is there in that legend?" Tau asked.

The Chief Ranger shrugged. "Who can say? This much *is* true: I have served my life in the forests since I could walk. I have listened to the talk of Trackers, Hunters, Rangers in my father's courtyards and field camps since I could understand their words. Yet never has any man reported the finding of a body of a graz that died a natural death. The scavengers might well account for the bulk of flesh, but the tusks and the bones should be visible for years. And this, too, I have seen with my own eyes: a graz close to death, supported by two of its kind and being urged along to the big swamps. Perhaps it is only that the suffering animal longs for water at its end, or perhaps in the heart of that morass there does lie the graz graveyard. But no man has found a naturally dead graz nor has any returned from exploring the big swamps. . . ."

Lightning on peaks which were like polished jet—bare rock above, the lush overgrowth of jungle below. And between, this fortress held by men who dared both the heights and the depths. The wildly burgeoning life of Khatka had surrounded the off-worlders since they had come here. There was something untameable about Khatka; the lush planet lured and yet repelled at the same time.

"Zoboru far from here?"

The Chief Ranger pointed north in answer to the captain's question.

"About a hundred leagues. It is the first new preserve we have prepared in ten years. And it is our desire to make it the best for tri-dee hunters. That is why we are now operating taming teams—"

"Taming teams?" Dane had to ask.

The Chief Ranger was ready enough to discuss his project.

"Zoboru is a no-kill preserve. The animals, they come to learn that after a while. But we cannot wait several years until they do. So we make them gifts." He laughed, evidently recalling some incident. "Sometimes, perhaps, we are too eager. Most of our visitors who wish to make tri-dees want to picture big game—graz, amplet, rock apes, lions—"

"Lions?" echoed Dane.

"Not Terran lions, no. But my people, when they landed on Khatka, found a few animals that reminded them of those they had always known. So they gave those the same names. A Khatkan lion is furred, it is a hunter and a great fighter, but it not the cat of Terra. However, it is in great demand as a tri-dee actor. So we summon it out of lurking by providing free meals. One shoots a poli, a water rat, or a landeer and drags the carcass behind a low-flying flitter. The lion springs upon the moving meat, which it can also scent, and the rope is cut, leaving a free dinner.

"The lions are not stupid. In a very short time they connect the sound of a flitter cutting the air with food. So they come to the banquet and those on the flitter can take their tridee shots at ease. Only there must also be care taken in such training. One forest guard on the Komog preserve became too enterprising. He dragged his kill at first. Then, to see if he could get the lions to forget man's presence entirely, he hung the training carcasses on the flitter, encouraging them to jump for their food.

"For the guard that was safe enough, but it worked too too well. A month or so later a Hunter was escorting a client through Komog and they swung low to get a good picture of a water rat emerging from the river. Suddenly there was a snarl behind them and they found themselves sharing the flitter with a lioness annoyed at finding no meat waiting on board.

"Luckily, they both wore stass belts; but they had to land the flitter and leave until the lioness wandered off, and she seriously damaged the machine in her irritation. So now our guards play no more fancy tricks while on taming runs. Tomorrow—no," he corrected himself, "the day after tomorrow I will be able to show you how the process works."

"And tomorrow?" inquired the captain.

"Tomorrow my men make hunting magic." Asaki's voice was expressionless.

"Your chief witch doctor being?" questioned Tau.

"Lumbrilo." The Chief Ranger did not appear disposed to add to that but Tau pursued the subject.

"His office is hereditary?"

"Yes. Does that make any difference?" For the first time there was a current of repressed eagerness in the other's tone.

"Perhaps a vast amount of difference," Tau replied. "A heriditary office may carry with it two forms of conditioning, one to influence its holder, one to affect the public-at-large. Your Lumbrilo may have come to believe deeply in his own powers; he would be a very remarkable man if he did not. It is almost certain that your people unquestionably accept him as a worker of wonders?"

"They do so accept." Once more Asaki's voice was drained of life.

"And Lumbrilo does not accept something you believe necessary?"

"Again the truth, Medic. Lumbrilo does not accept his proper place in the scheme of things!"

"He is a member of one of your Five Families?"

"No, his clan is small, always set apart. From the beginning here, those who spoke for gods and demons did not also order men."

"Separation of church and state," commented Tau thoughtfully. "Yet in our Terran past there have been times when church and state were one. Does Lumbrilo desire that?"

Asaki raised his eyes to the mountain peaks, to the northward where lay his beloved work.

"I do not know what Lumbrilo wants, save that it makes mischief—or worse! This I tell you: hunting magic is part of our lives and it has at its core some of those unexplainable happenings which you have acknowledged do exist. I have used powers I can neither explain nor understand as part of my work. In the jungle and on the grasslands an off-worlder must guard his life with a stass belt if he goes unarmed. But I—any of my men—can walk unharmed if we obey the rules of our magic. Only Lumbrilo does other things which his forefathers did not. And he boasts that he can do more. So he has a growing following of those who believe—and those who fear."

"You want me to face him?"

The Chief Ranger's big hands closed upon the rim of the parapet as if they could exert enough pressure to crumble the hard stone. "I want you to see whether there is trickery in this. Trickery I can fight, for that there are weapons. But if Lumbrilo truly controls forces for which there is no name, then perhaps we must patch up an uneasy peace—or go down in defeat. And, off-worlder, I come from a line of warriors—we do not drink defeat easily!"

"That I also believe," Tau returned quietly. "Be sure, sir, if there is trickery in this man's magic and I can detect it, the secret shall be yours."

"Let us hope that so it shall be."

Subconsciously, Dane had always associated the practice of magic with darkness and the night. But the next morning the sun was high and hot when he made one of the party coming down to a second and larger walled terrace where the Hunters, Trackers, Guards and other followers of the Chief Ranger were assembled in irregular rows.

There was a low sound which was more a throb in the clear air about them, getting into a man's blood and pumping in rhythm there. Dane tracked the sound to its source: four large drums standing waist high before the men who tapped them delicately with the tips of all ten fingers.

The necklaces of claws and teeth about those dusky throats, the kilts of fringed hide, the crossed belts of brilliantly spotted or striped fur were in contrast to the very efficient and modern side arms each man wore, to the rest of the equipment sheathed and strapped at their belts.

There was a carved stool for the Chief Ranger, another for Captain Jellico. Dane and Tau settled themselves on the less comfortable seats of the terrace steps. Those tapping fingers increased their rate of beat, and the notes of the drums rose from the low murmur of hived bees to the mutter of mountain thunder still half a range away. A bird called from those inner courts of the palace from which the women never ventured.

Da—da—da—da . . . Voices took up the thud-thud of the drums; the heads of the squatting men moved in a slow swing from side to side. Tau's hand closed about Dane's wrist and the younger man looked around, startled, to see that the medic's eyes were alight, that he was watching the assembly with the alertness of Sindbad approaching prey.

"Calculate the stowage space in Number One hold!"

That amazing order, delivered in a whisper, shocked Dane into obeying it. Number One hold . . . there were three divisions now and the stowage was— He became aware that for a small space of time he had escaped the net being woven by the beat of the drum, the drone of voices, the nodding of heads. He moistened his lips. So that was how it worked! He had heard Tau speak often enough about self-hypnotism under such conditions, but this was the first time the meaning of it had been clear.

Two men were shuffling out of nowhere, wearing nothing on their dark bodies but calf-length kilts of tails, black tails with fluffy white tips, which swayed uniformly in time to their pacing feet. Their heads and shoulders were masked by beautifully cured and semi-mounted animal heads displaying half-open jaws with double pairs of curved fangs.

The black-and-white striped fur, the sharply pointed ears, were neither canine nor feline, but a weird combination of the two.

Dane gabbled two trading formulas under his breath and tried to think of the relation of Samantine rock coinage to galactic credits. Only this time his defenses did not work. From between the two shuffling dancers padded something on four feet. The canine-feline creature was more than just a head; it was a loose-limbed, graceful body fully eight feet in length, and the red eyes in the prick-eared head were those of a confident killer. It walked without restraint, lazily, with arrogance, its white-tufted tail swinging. And when it reached the mid-point of the terrace, it flung up its head as if to challenge. But words issued from between those curved fangs, words which Dane might not understand but which undoubtedly held meaning for the men nodding in time to the hypnotic cadence of that da—da—da . . .

"Beautiful!" Tau spoke in honest admiration, his own eyes almost as feral as those of the talking beast as he leaned forward, his fists on his knees.

Now the animal was dancing also, its paws following the pace set by the masked attendants. It must be a man in an animal skin. But Dane could hardly believe that. The illusion was too perfect. His own hands went to the knife sheath at his belt. Out of deference to local custom they had left their stun rods in the palace, but a belt knife was an accepted article of apparel. Dane slid the blade out surreptitiously, setting its point against the palm of his hand and jabbing painfully. This was another of Tau's answers for breaking a spell. But the white and black creature continued to dance; there was no blurring of its body lines into those of a human being.

It sang on in a high-pitched voice, and Dane noted that those of the audience nearest the stools where Asaki and the captain were seated now watched the Chief Ranger and the space officer. He felt Tau tense beside him.

"Trouble coming. . . . " The warning from Tau was the merest thread of sound. Dane forced himself to look away from the swaying cat-dog, to watch instead the singers who were now furtively eyeing their lord and his guest. The Terran knew that there were feudal bonds between the Ranger and his men. But suppose this was a showdown between Lumbrilo and Asaki—whose side would these men take?

He watched Captain Jellico's hand slide across his knee, his fingers drop in touching distance of knife hilt. And the hand of the Chief Ranger, hanging lax at his side, suddenly balled into a fist.

"So!" Tau expelled the word as a hiss. He moved with sure-footed speed. Now he passed between the stools to confront the dancing cat-dog. Yet he did not look at that weird creature and its attendants. Instead his arms were flung high as if to ward off—or perhaps welcome—something on the mountain side as he shouted:

"Hodi, eldama! Hodi!"

As one, those on the terrace turned, looked up toward the slope. Dane was on his feet, holding his knife as he might a sword. Though of what use its puny length would be against that huge bulk moving in slow majesty toward them, he did not try to think.

Gray-dark trunk curled upward between great ivory tusks, ears went wide as ponderous feet crunched volcanic soil. Tau moved forward, his hand still upraised, clearly in greeting. That trunk touched skyward as if in salute to the man who could be crushed under one foot.

"Hodi, eldama!" For the second time Tau hailed the monster elephant and the trunk raised in silent greeting from one lord of an earth to another he recognized as an equal. Perhaps it had been a thousand years since man and elephant had stood so, and then there had been only war and death between them. Now there was peace and a current of power flowing from one to the other. Dane sensed this, saw the men on the terrace likewise drawing back from the unseen tie between the medic and the bull he had so clearly summoned.

Then Tau's upheld hands came together in a sharp clap and men held their breath in wonder. Where the great bull had stood there was nothing—except rocks in the sun.

As Tau swung around to face the cat-dog, that creature had no substance either. For he fronted no animal but a man, a small, lean man whose lips wrinkled back from his teeth in a snarl. His attendant priests fell back, leaving the spaceman and the witch doctor alone.

"Lumbrilo's magic is great," Tau said evenly. "I hail Lumbrilo of Khatka." His hand made the open-palmed salute of peace.

The snarl faded as the man brought his face under control. He stood naked, but he was clothed in inherent dignity. And there was power with that dignity, power and a pride before which even the more physically impressive Chief Ranger might have to give place.

"You have magic also, outlander," he replied. "Where walks this long-toothed shadow of yours now?"

"Where once the men of Khatka walked, Lumbrilo. For it was men of your blood who long, long past hunted this shadow of mine and made its body their prey."

"So that it now might have a blood debt to settle with us, outlander?"

"That you said, not I, man of power. You have shown us one beast, I have shown another. Who can say which of them is stronger when it issues forth from the shadows?"

Lumbrilo pattered forward, his bare feet making little sound on the stones of the terrace. Now he was only an arm's-length away from the medic.

"You have challenged me, off-world man." Was that a question or a statement? Dane wondered.

"Why should I challenge you, Lumbrilo? To each race its own magic. I come not to offer battle." His eyes held steady with the Khatkan's

"You have challenged me." Lumbrilo turned away and then looked back over his shoulder. "The strength you depend upon may become a broken staff, off-worlder. Remember my words in the time when shadows become substance, and substance the thinnest of shadows!"

III

"YOU ARE truly a man of power!"

Tau shook his head in answer to that outburst from Asaki.

"Not so, sir. Your Lumbrilo is a man of power. I drew upon his power and you saw the results."

"Deny it not! What we saw never walked this world."

Tau slung the strap of a trail bag over his shoulder. "Sir, once men of your blood, men who bred your race, hunted the elephant. They took his tusks for their treasure, feasted upon his flesh—yes, and died beneath the trampling of his feet when they were unlucky or unwary. So there is that within you which can even now be awakened to remember *eldama* in his might when he was king of the herd and need fear nothing save the spears and cunning of small, weak men. Lumbrilo had already awakened your minds to see what he willed you to see."

"How does he do this?" asked the other simply. "Is it magic that we see not Lumbrilo but a lion before us?"

"He waves his spell with the drums, with the chant, by the suggestion his mind imposes upon yours. And, having woven his spell, he cannot limit it to just the picture he suggests if ancient racial memories raise another. I merely used the tools of Lumbrilo to show you yet another picture your people once knew well."

"And in so doing made an enemy." Asaki stood before a rack of very modern weapons. Now he made his selection, a silver tube with a stock curved to fit a man's shoulder. "Lumbrilo will not forget."

Tau laughed shortly. "No, but then I have merely done as you wished, have I not, sir? I have focused on myself the enmity of a dangerous man, and now you hope I shall be forced, in self-defense, to remove him from your path."

The Khatkan turned slowly, resting the weapon across his forearm. "I do not deny that, spaceman."

"Then matters here are indeed serious—"

"They are so serious," Asaki interrupted, speaking not only to Tau but to the other off-worlders as well, "that what happens now may mean the end of the Khatka that I know. Lumbrilo is the most dangerous game I have faced in a lifetime as a hunter. He goes, or we draw his fangs—or else all that I am, all I have labored here to build, will be swept away. To preserve this I will use any weapon."

"And I am now your weapon, which you hope will be as successful as that needler you are carrying." Tau laughed again, without much humor. "Let us hope I shall prove as effective."

Jellico moved out of the shadows. It was just after dawn, and the grayness of the vanishing night still held in the corners of the armory. Deliberately he took his own stand before the arms racks and chose a short-barreled blaster. Only when its butt was cupped in his hand did he glance at his host.

"We came guesting, Asaki. We have eaten salt and bread under this roof."

"On my body and my blood it is," returned the Khatkan grimly. "I shall go down to the blackness of Sabra before you do, if the flames of death are against us." From his belt he flipped loose his knife and offered the hilt to Jellico. "My body for a wall between you and the dark, Captain. But also understand this: to me, what I do now is greater than the life of any one man. Lumbrilo and the evil behind him must be rooted out. There was no trickery in my invitation!"

They stood eye to eye, equal in height, in authority of person, and that indefinable something which made them both masters in their own different worlds. Then Jellico's hand went out, his fingertip flicked the hilt of the bared blade.

"There was no trickery," he conceded. "I knew that your need was great when you came to the *Queen*."

Since both the captain and Tau appeared to accept the situation, Dane, not quite understanding it all, was prepared to follow their lead. And for the moment they had nothing more in plan than to visit the Zoboru preserve.

They went by flitter—Asaki, one of his Hunter pilots, and the three from the *Queen*—lifting over the rim of mountains behind the fortress-palace and speeding north with the rising sun a flaming ball to the east. Below, the country was stark —rocks and peaks, deep purple shadows marking the veins of crevices. But that was swiftly behind and they were over a sea of greens, many shades of green, with yellow, blue, even red cutting into the general verdant carpet of treetops. Another chain of heights and then open land, swales of tall grass already burnt yellow by the steady sun. There was a river here, a crazy, twisted stream coiling nearly back upon itself at times.

Once more broken land, land so ravished by prehistoric volcanic action that it was a grotesque nightmare of erosion-whittled outcrops and mesas. Asaki pointed out into a vast wedge. There was a dark patch widening out into a vast wedge.

"The swamp of Mygra. It has not yet been explored."

"You could air map it," Tau began.

The Chief Ranger was frowning. "Four flitters have been lost trying that. Com reports fail when they cross that last mountain ridge eastward. There is some sort of interference which we do not yet understand. Mygra is a place of death; later we may be able to travel along its fringe and then you shall see. Now—" He spoke to the pilot in his own tongue and the flitter pointed up-nose at an angle as they climbed over the highest peak they had yet seen in this mountainous land, to reach at last a country of open grass dotted with small forest stands. Jellico nodded approvingly.

"Zoboru?"

"Zoboru," Asaki assented. "We shall go up to the northern end of the preserve. I wish to show you the roosts of the fastals. This is their nesting season and the sight is one you will long remember. But we shall take an eastern course; I have two Ranger stations to check on the way."

It was after they left the second station that the flitter swung farther out eastward, again climbing over the chain of heights to sight one of the newly discovered wonders the staff at the last station had reported—a crater lake.

And the flitter skimmed down across water which was a rich emerald in hue, filling the crater from one rock wall to the other with no beach at the foot of those precipitant cliffs. As the machine arose to clear the far wall, Dane tensed. One of his duties aboard the *Queen* was flitter pilot for planet-wise trips. And ever since they had taken off that morning he had unconsciously flown with the Khatkan pilot, anticipating each change or adjustment of the controls. Now he felt that sluggish response to the other's lift signal, and instinctively his own hand went out to adjust a power feed lever.

They made the rise, were well above the danger of the cliff wall. But the machine was not responding properly. Dane did not need to watch the pilot's swiftly moving hands to guess that they were in trouble. And his slight concern deepened into something else as the flitter began to drop nose again. In front of him, Captain Jellico shifted uneasily, and Dane knew that he, too, was alerted.

Now the pilot had plunged the power adjuster to the head against the control board. But the nose of the flitter acted as if it were overweighted or magnetically attracted by the rocks below. The best efforts of the man flying it could not keep it level. They were being drawn earthward, and all the pilot could do only delayed the inevitable crack-up. The Khatkan was turning the machine north to avoid what lay below, for here a long arm of the Mygra swamp clasped about the foot of the mountain.

The Chief Ranger spoke into the mike of the com unit while the pilot continued to fight against the pull which was bringing then down. Now the small machine was below the level of the volcanic peak which cradled the lake, and the mountain lay between them and the preserve.

Asaki gave a muffled exclamation, slapped the com box, spoke more sharply into the mike. It was apparent he was not getting the results he wanted. Then with a quick glance about he snapped an order:

"Strap in!"

His Terran companions had already buckled the wide webbing belts intended to save them from crash shock. Dane saw the pilot push the button to release fend cushions. In spite of his pounding heart, a small fraction of his brain recognized the other's skill as the Khatkan took a course to bring them down on a relatively level patch of sand and gravel.

Dane raised his head from the shelter of his folded arms. The Chief Ranger was busy with the pilot, who lay limply against the controls. Captain Jellico and Tau were already pulling at the buckles of their protective crash belts. But one look at the front of the flitter told Dane that it would not take to the air again without extensive repairs. Its nose was bent up and back, obscuring the forward view completely. However, the pilot had made a miraculously safe landing considering the terrain.

Ten minutes later, the pilot restored to consciousness and the gash in his head bandaged, they held a council of war.

"The com was off, too. I did not have a chance to report before the crash," Asaki put the situation straightly. "And our exploring parties have not yet mapped this side of the range; it has a bad reputation because of the swamp."

Jellico measured the heights now to their west with resigned eyes. "Looks as if we climb."

"Not here," the Chief Ranger corrected him. "There is no passing through the crater lake region on foot. We must travel south along the edge of the mountain area until we do find a scalable way into the preserve region."

"You seem very certain we are not going to be rescued if we stay right here," Tau observed. "Why?"

"Because I'm inclined to believe that any flitter that tries to reach us may run into the same trouble. Also, they have no com fix on us. It will be at least a day or more before they will even begin to count us missing, and then they will have the whole northern portion of the preserve to comb; there are not enough men here—I can give you a multitude of reasons, Medic."

"One of which might be sabotage?" demanded Jellico.

Asaki shrugged. "Perhaps. I am not loved in some quarters. But there may also be something fatal to flitters here as there is over Mygra. We thought the crater lake district safely beyond the swamp influence, but it may not be so."

But you took the chance of traveling over it, Dane thought, though he did not comment aloud. Was this another of the Chief Ranger's attempts to involve them in some private trouble of his own? Though to deliberately smash up a flitter and set them all afoot in this wilderness was a pretty drastic move.

Asaki had started to unload emergency supplies from the flitter. They each had a trail bag for a pack. But when the pilot staggered over to pull out a set of stass belts and Jellico began to uncoil them, the Chief Ranger shook his head.

"With the feeder beam shut off by the mountains, I fear those will no longer work."

Jellico tossed one on the crumpled nose of the flitter and

punched its button with the tip of the needler barrel. Then he threw a rock at the dangling belt. The stone landed, taking the wide protective band with it to the ground. That force field which should have warded off the missive was not working.

"Oh, fine!" Tau opened his trail bag to pack concentrates. Then he smiled crookedly. "We aren't signed in for killing licenses, sir. Do you pay our fines if we are forced to shoot a hole through something that disputes the right of way?"

To Dane's surprise, the Chief Ranger laughed. "You are off preserve now, Medic Tau. The rules do not cover wild land. But I would suggest we now hunt a cave before nightfall."

"Lions?" asked Jellico.

Dane, remembering the black and white beast Lumbrilo had presented, did not enjoy that thought. They had—his gaze went from man to man checking weapons—the needler Asaki carried, and another the pilot had slung by its carrying strap over his shoulder. Tau and the captain both were armed with blasters and he had a fire ray and a force blade, both considered small arms but deadly enough perhaps even to dampen a lion's enthusiasm for the chase.

"Lions, graz, rock apes." Asaki fastened the mouth of his trail bag. "All are hunters or killers. The graz send out scouts, and they are big and formidable enough to have no enemies. Lions hunt with intelligence and skill. Rock apes are dangerous, but luckily they cannot keep silent when they scent their prey and so give one warning."

As they climbed up-slope from the flitter, Dane, looking back, saw that perhaps Asaki was right in his belief that they had better try to help themselves rather than wait for rescue. Putting aside the excuse of fearing another crack-up, the wrecked flitter made no outstanding mark on the ground. The higher they climbed, the less it could be distinguished from the tumble of rocks about it.

He had lagged a little behind and, when he hurried to catch up, found Jellico standing with his distance vision lenses to his eyes, directing them toward that shadow marking the swamp. As the younger spaceman reached him, the captain lowered the glasses and spoke:

"Take your knife, Thorson, and hold it close to that rock—

over there." He pointed to a rounded black knob protruding from the soil a little off their path.

Dane obeyed, only to have the blade jerk in his hand. And when he loosened his hold in amazement, the steel slapped tight against the stone.

"Magnetic!"

"Yes. Which might explain our crash. Also this." Jellico held out a field compass to demonstrate that its needle had gone completely mad.

"We can use the mountain range itself for a guide," Dane said with more confidence than he felt.

"True enough. But we may have trouble when we head west again." Jellico let the lenses swing free on their cord about his neck. "If we were wrecked on purpose"—his mouth tightened and the old blaster burn on his cheek stretched as did his jaw set—"then someone is going to answer a lot of questions—and fast!"

"The Chief Ranger, sir?"

"I don't know. I just don't know!" The captain grunted as he adjusted his pack and started on.

If fortune had failed them earlier, she smiled on them now. Asaki discovered a cave before sundown, located not too far from a mountain stream. The Ranger sniffed the air before that dark opening as the Hunter pilot shed his equipment and crept forward on his hands and knees, his head up and his nostrils expanding as he, too, tested the scent from the cave mouth.

Scent? It was closer to a stench, and one ripe enough to turn the stomach of an off-worlder. But the Hunter glanced back over his shoulder and nodded reassuringly.

"Lion. But old. Not here within five days at least."

"Well enough. And even old lion scent will keep away rock apes. We'll clean some and then we can rest undisturbed," was his superior's comment.

The cleaning was easy, for the brittle bedding of dried bracken and grass the beast had left burned quickly, cleansing with both fire and smoke. When they raked the ashes out with branches, Asaki and Nymani brought in handfuls of leaves which they crumpled and threw on the floor, spreading an aromatic odor which banished most of the foulness.

Dane, at the stream with the canteens to fill, chanced upon a small pool where there was a spread of smooth yellow sand.

Knowing well the many weird booby traps one might stumble into on a strange world, the Terran prospected carefully, stirring up the stand with a stick. Sighting not so much as a water insect or a curious fish, he pulled off his boots, rolled up his breeches and waded in. The water was cool and refreshing, though he dared not drink it until the purifier was added. Then, with the filled canteens knotted together by their straps, he put on his boots and climbed to the cave where Tau waited with water tablets.

Half an hour later Dane sat cross-legged by the fire, turning a spit strung with three small birds Asaki had brought in. One foot closer to the heat began to tingle and he eased off his boot, his cramped toes suddenly seeming to have doubled in size. He was staring wide-eyed at these same toes, puffed, red, and increasingly painful to the touch, when Nymani squatted beside him, inspected his foot closely, and ordered him to take off his other boot.

"What is it?" Dane found that shedding the other boot was a minor torture in itself.

Nymani was cutting tiny splinters, hardly thicker than a needle, from a stick.

"Sand worm—lays eggs in flesh. We burn them out or you have bad foot."

"Burn them out!" Dane echoed, and then swallowed as he watched Nymani advance a splinter to the fire.

"Burn them," the Khatkan repeated firmly. "Burn tonight, hurt some tomorrow; all well soon. No burn—very bad."

Dane ruefully prepared to pay the consequences of his first brush with the unpleasant surprises Khatka had to offer.

IV

DANE REGARDED his throbbing feet morosely. Nymani's operations with burning splinters had been hard to take, but he had endured them without disgracing himself before the

Khatkans, who appeared to regard such a mishap as just another travel incident. Now, with Tau's salve soothing the worst of the after effects, the Terran was given time to reflect upon his own stupidity and the fact that he might now prove a drag on the whole party the next morning.

"That's queer. . . ."

Dane was startled out of the contemplation of his misery to see the medic on his knees before their row of canteens, the vial of water purifier held to the firelight for a closer inspection.

"What's the matter?"

"We must have hit with a pretty hard thump back there. Some of these pills are powder! Have to guess about the portion to add." With the tip of his knife blade Tau scraped a tiny amount of pill fragments into each waiting canteen. "That should do it. But if the water tastes a little bitter, don't let it bother you."

Bitter water, Dane thought, trying to flex his still swollen toes, was going to be the least of his worries in the morning. But he determined that his boots should go on at daybreak, and he would keep on his feet as long as the others did, no matter how much it cost him.

And when they set out shortly after daybreak, wanting to move as far as they could before the heat hours when they must rest, the going was not too bad. Dane's feet were tender to the touch, but he could shuffle along at the tail of the procession with only Nymani playing rear guard behind him.

Jungle lay before them and bush knives began to swing, clearing their path. Dane took his turn with the rest at that chore, thankful that the business of cutting their way through that mass of greenery slowed them to a pace he could match —if not in comfort, then by willpower.

But the sand worms were not the only troubles one could encounter on Khatka. Within an hour Captain Jellico stood sweating and speaking his mind freely in the native tongues of five different planets while Tau and Nymani worked as a team with skinning knives. They were not flaying the spaceman, but they came near to that in places as they worried a choice selection of tree thorns out of his arm and shoulder. The captain had been unfortunate enough to trip and fall into the embrace of a very unfriendly bush.

Dane inspected a fallen tree for evidence of inimical wild

life, and then rested his blanket between him and it as a protecting cushion before he sat down. These trees were not the towering giants of the true forests, but rather oversized bushes which had been made into walls by twined vines. Brilliant bursts of flowers were splotches of vivid color, and the attendant insect life was altogether too abundant. Dane tried to tally his immunity shots and hoped for the best. At the moment he wondered why anyone would want to visit Khatka, let alone pay some astronomical sum for the privilege. Though he could also guess that the plush safari arranged for a paying client might be run on quite different lines from their own present trek.

How *could* a tracker find his way through this? With the compasses playing crazy tricks into the bargain! Jellico knew that the compasses were off, yet the captain had followed Asaki's lead without question, so he must trust the Ranger's forest craft. But Dane wished they were clear on the mountain side again.

Time had little meaning in that green gloom. But when they worked through to meet rock walls again, the sun said it was well into the after part of the day. They sheltered for a breather under the drooping limbs of one of the last trees.

"Amazing!" Jellico, his torn arm in a sling across his chest, came down-slope from the higher point where he had been using the distance lenses. "We struck straight across and cut off about ten miles by that jungle jog. Now I believe all that I've heard of your people's ability to cross wilderness and not lose their built in 'riding beams,' sir. With the compasses out, I'll admit I've been nourishing a healthy set of doubts."

Asaki laughed. "Captain, I do not question your ability to flit from world to world, or how you have learned to set up trade with strange humans and non-humans alike. To each his own mystery. On Khatka every boy before he becomes a man must learn to navigate the jungle, and with no instruments to help him, only what lies in here." He touched his thumb to his forehead. "So through generations we have developed our homing instincts. Those who did not, also did not live to father others who might have had the same lack. We are hounds who can run on a scent, and we are migrators who have better than a compass within our own bodies."

"Now we take to climbing again?" Tau surveyed the way before them critically.

"Not at this hour. That sun on the upward slopes can cook a man's skin were he to touch any rock. We wait. . . ."

Waiting for the Khatkans was a chance to sleep. They curled up on their light blankets. But the three spacemen were restless. Dane would have liked to have taken off his boots, but feared he could not replace them; and he could tell from the way the captain shifted his position that Jellico was in pain too. Tau sat quietly, staring at nothing Dane could see, unless it was a tall rock thrust out of the slope like a finger pointing skyward.

"What color is that rock?"

Surprised, Dane gave the stony finger closer attention. To him it was the same color as most of the other rocks, a weathered black which in certain lights appeared to carry a brownish film.

"Black, or maybe dark brown."

Tau looked past him to Jellico. The captain nodded. "I'd agree with that."

Tau cupped his hands over his eyes for a moment and his lips moved as if he were counting. Then he took his hands away and stared up-slope. Dane watched the medic's eyelids blink slowly. "Nothing but black or brown?" Tau pressed.

"No." Jellico supported his injured arm upon his knees, leaning forward, as intent upon the designated rock as if he expected it to assume some far more startling appearance.

"Queer," Tau said to himself, and then added briskly, "You're right, of course. That sun can play tricks with one's eyes."

Dane continued to watch the finger rock. Maybe strong sunlight could play tricks, but he could see nothing odd about that rough lump. And since the captain asked no questions of Tau, he did not quite want to either.

It was perhaps a half-hour later, and the medic and Jellico had both succumbed to the quiet, the heat, and their own fatigue, when Dane did sight a movement up-slope. The throbbing in his feet was worse now that he had nothing to occupy his mind but his own troubles, and he was sitting facing the finger rock.

Was that what Tau had seen earlier? That quick movement around the side of the rough pillar? But if so, why the question of color? There it was again! And now, centering all his attention on that one point, the Terran picked out the outline of a head—a head grotesque enough to be something conjured out of Lumbrilo's sorcerer's imagination. Had Dane not seen its like among the tri-dee prints in Captain Jellico's collection, he would have believed that his eyes were playing tricks.

It was a bullet-shaped head, embellished by two out-sized prick ears, the hair-tufted pointed tips of which projected well above the top of the skull. Round eyes were set deeply in sunken pits. The mouth was a swinish snout from which lolled a purple tongue, though the rest of that gargoyle head was very close in color to the rock against which it half rested.

Dane had no doubts that the rock ape was spying upon the small camp. Having heard tales of those semi-intelligent animals—the most intelligent native creatures of Khatka—most of which were concerned with their more malignant characteristics, Dane was alarmed. That lurker could be an advance scout of some pack. And a pack of rock apes, if able to surprise their prey, were formidable opponents.

Asaki stirred, sat up. And that round head above turned to follow the Chief Ranger's every move.

"Above . . . by the finger rock . . . to the right . . ." Dane kept his voice close to a whisper. When he saw the sudden constriction of muscle across the Khatkan's bare shoulders, he knew that the other had heard and understood.

Only, if Asaki had spotted the rock ape, he did not betray his knowledge. The Khatkan got lithely to his feet. Then one of those feet stirred Nymani into the instant wakefulness of the wilderness-trained man.

Dane slid his hand about the bole of the tree and touched Jellico, watched the captain's gray eyes open with a similar awareness. Asaki picked up his needler. Weapon in hand, he whirled and fired almost in one connected movement. It was the fastest shot Dane had ever seen.

The gargoyle head lifted away from the rock, and then turned to one side as its body, somehow vaguely obscene in its resemblance to the human form, fell away, to sprawl limply down-slope.

Though the dead rock ape had not had a chance to give tongue, there came a cry from above, a coughing, deep-throated hawking. Down the steep incline bumped a round white ball, bouncing past the tumbled carcass of the ape, sailing up into the air, to strike and burst open a few feet away.

"Back!" With one arm Asaki sent Jellico, his nearest neighbor, tumbling back into the jungle. Then the Chief Ranger pumped a stream of needle rays into the remains of the ball. A shrill, sweet humming arose as red motes, vivid as molten copper in the sunlight, climbed on wings beating too fast to be seen.

The debris of the nest smoked into nothing. But no needle ray could hope to stop all the poisonous army issuing forth from it, fighting mad, to seek any warm-blooded creature within scenting distance. The men threw themselves into the brush, rolling in the thick mold of the vegetable decay on the ground, rubbing its moist plaster over their bodies in frantic haste.

Red-hot fire, far worse than any of the splinter torment Dane had undergone the night before, pierced between his shoulders. He rolled on his back, shoving himself along, both to kill the fire-wasp and coat the sting with cooling mold. Cries of pain told him that he was not the only sufferer, as all dug hands into the slimy stuff under them and slapped it over their faces and heads.

"Apes. . . ." That half shout got through to alert the men on the jungle floor. True to their nature, the rock apes, now streaming downhill, were coughing their challenges, advertising their attack. And it was only that peculiarity of their species which saved their intended victims.

The apes came forward, partially erect, at a shambling run. The first two, bulls close to six feet, went down under fire from Asaki's needler. A third somehow escaped, swerving to the left, and came bounding at an angle toward Dane. The Terran jerked free his force blade as that swine snout split wide to show greenish tusks and the horrible stench of the creature's body made him gasp.

A taloned paw clawed at him eagerly, slipped from his slime-covered body just as he brought the force blade up. Foul breath coughed in his face and he stumbled back as the heavy body of the ape crashed against him, cut in half by the weapon. To Dane's sickened horror the paws still clawed for him, the fangs still gnashed as he rolled free of the mangled body and somehow got to his feet.

The roar of a blaster, of two blasters, drowned out the

clamor of the apes as Dane drew his fire ray, set his shoulders against a tree bole and prepared to fight it out. He fired, saw a smaller and more nimble enemy go down screeching. Then there were none left on their shaggy feet, though some on the ground dragged themselves forward, still striving to reach the men.

Dane slapped a fire-wasp from his leg. He was glad of the support of the tree at his back as the smell of the ape's blood drenching him from chest level down, and the mess on the ground, made his stomach churn.

When he could control his retching, he straightened. To his relief he saw that all the others were on their feet, apparently unharmed. But, Tau, catching sight of the younger spaceman, gasped and started for him.

"Dane! What did they do?"

His junior laughed a little hysterically. "Not mine. . . ." He swabbed with a handful of grass at his bloodied breeches and blundered on into the sunlight.

Nymani found them a foam-flecked stream below a miniature falls where the swift current prevented the lurking of sand worms. They stripped eagerly, cleaning first themselves and then their fouled clothing while Tau tended the wealth of fire-wasp stings. There was little he could do to relieve the swelling and pain, until Asaki produced a reed-like plant which, chopped in sections, yielded a sticky purple liquid that dried on the skin as a tar gum—the native remedy. So, glued and plastered, they climbed away from the water and prepared to spend the night in a hollow between two leaning rocks, certainly not as snug as the cave but a fortress of sorts.

"And credit-happy space hoppers pay a fortune for an outing like this!" Tau commented bitterly, hunching well forward so that a certain stung portion of his anatomy would not come in contact with the rock beneath him.

"Hardly for this," Jellico replied, and Dane saw Nymani grin one-sidedly, his other cheek puffed and painted sticky purple.

"We do not always encounter apes and fire-wasps in the same day," supplied the Chief Ranger. "Also, guests at the preserves wear stass belts."

Jellico snorted. "I don't think you'd get any repeats from your clients otherwise! What do we meet tomorrow? A herd f graz on stampede, or something even more subtle and leadly?"

Nymani got up and walked a little way from their rock shelter. He turned down-slope and Dane saw his nostrils expand as they had when he had investigated the cave.

"Something is dead," he said slowly. "A very large something. Or else—"

Asaki strode down to join his men. He gave a curt nod and Nymani skidded on down the mountain side.

"What is it?" Jellico asked.

"It might be many things. There is one I hope it is not," was the Chief Ranger's somewhat evasive reply. "I will hunt a labbla—there was fresh spoor at the stream." He set off long their back trail to return a half hour later, the body of his kill slung across one shoulder. He was skinning it when Nymani trotted back.

"Well?"

"Death pit," supplied the Hunter.

"Poachers?" Jellico inquired.

Nymani nodded. Asaki continued his task, but there was a glint in his dark eyes as he butchered with sure and expert strokes. Then he glanced at the shadow extending beyond the rocks.

"I, too, would see," he told Nymani.

Jellico arose, and Dane, interested, followed. Some five minutes later none of them needed the native keenness of smell to detect the presence of some foulness ahead. The odor of corruption was almost tangible in the sultry air. And it grew worse until they stood on the edge of a pit. Dane retreated hurriedly. This was as bad as the battlefield of the rock apes. But the captain and the two Khatkans stood calmly assessing the slaughter left by the hide poachers.

"Clam, graz, hoodra," Jellico commented. "Tusks and hides —the full line of trade stuff."

Asaki, his expression bleak, stepped back from the pit. "Day old calves, old ones, females—all together. They kill wantonly and leave those they do not choose to pelt."

"Trail—" Nymani pointed eastward. "Leads to Mygra swamp."

"The swamps!" Asaki was shaken. "They must be mad!"

"Or know more about this country than your men do," Jellico corrected.

"If poachers can enter Mygra, then we can follow!"

But not now, Dane protested silently. Certainly Asaki did not mean that *they* were to track outlaws into swamps the Khatkan had already labeled unexplored death traps!

V

SITTING UP, Dane stared wide-eyed into the dark. A handful of glowing coals, guarded by rocks, was the center of their camp. He hunched up to that hardly knowing why he moved. His hands were shaking, his skin damp with sweat no heat produced. Yet, now that he was conscious of the night, the Terran could not remember the nightmare from which he had just awakened, though he was left with a growing apprehension which he could not define. What prowled out there in that dark? Walked the mountain side? Listened, spied and waited?

Dane half started to his feet as a form did move into the dim light of the fire. Tau stood there, regarding him with sober intensity.

"Bad dream?"

The younger man admitted to that with a nod, partly against his will.

"Well, you aren't the only one. Remember any of it?"

With an effort, Dane looked away from the encircling dark. It was as if the fear which had shaken him awake, now embodied, lurked right there.

"No." He rubbed sleep-smarting eyes.

"Neither did I," Tau remarked. "But both of 'em must have been jet-powered."

"I suppose one could expect to have nightmares after yesterday." Dane advanced the logical explanation, yet at the same time something deep inside him denied every word of it. He had known nightmares before; none of them had left this aftertaste. And he wanted no return of sleep tonight. Reaching to the pile of wood he fed the fire as Tau settled down beside him.

"There is something else . . ." the medic began, and then fell silent. Dane did not press him. The younger man was too busy fighting a growing desire to whirl and aim the fire ray into that darkness, to catch in its withering blast that lurking thing he could *feel* padded there, biding its time.

Despite his efforts Dane did drowse again before morning, waking unrefreshed, and, to his secret dismay, with no lessening of his odd dislike for the country about them.

Asaki did not suggest that they trail the poachers into the morass of Mygra. Instead the Chief Ranger was eager to press on in the opposite direction, find a way over the range to the preserve where he could assemble a punitive force to deal with the outlaws. So they began an upward climb which took them away from the dank heat of the lowlands, into the parched blaze of the sunbaked ledges above.

The sun was bright, far too bright, and there were few shadows left. Yet Dane, stopping to drink sparingly from his canteen, could not lose that sense of eyes upon him, of being tracked. Rock apes? Cunning as those beasts were, it was against their nature to trail in utter silence, to be able to carry through a long-term project. Lion, perhaps?

He noted that Nymani and Asaki took turns at rear guard today, and that each was alert. Yet, oddly enough, none of them mentioned the uneasiness they must all share.

They had a dry climb, finding no mountain stream to renew their water supply. All being experienced in wilderness travel, they made a mouthful of liquid go a long way. When the party halted slightly before midday, canteens were still half full.

"*Haugh!*"

They jerked up, hands on weapons. A rock ape, its hideous body clearly seen here, capered, coughed, spat. Asaki fired from the hip and the thing screeched, clawed at its chest where the dark blood spewed out, and raced for them. Nymani cut the beast down and they waited tensely for the attack of the thing's tribe, which should have followed the abortive lunge on the part of their scout. But there was nothing—neither sound nor movement.

What did follow froze them all momentarily. That mangled body began to move again, drew itself together, crawled toward them. Dane knew that it was impossible that the creature could live with such wounds. Yet the beast advanced, its head lolling on its hunched shoulders so that the eyes were turned blindly up to the full glare of the sun, while it crawled to reach the man it could not see.

"Demon!" Nymani dropped his needler, shrank back against the rocks.

As the thing advanced, before their eyes the impossible happened. Those gaping wounds closed, the head straightened on the almost invisible neck, the eyes glared once more with life, and slaver dripped from the swine snout.

Jellico caught up the needler Nymani had dropped. With a coolness Dane envied, the captain shot. And for the second time the rock ape collapsed, torn to ribbons.

Nymani screamed, and Dane tried to choke back his own cry of horrified protest. The dead thing put on life for the second time, crawled, got somehow to its feet, healed itself, and came on. Asaki, his face greenish-pale, stepped out stiffly as if each step he took was forced by torture. He had dropped his needler. Now he caught up a rock as large as his own head, raised it high with arms on which the muscles stood out like ropes. He hurled the stone, and Dane heard as well as saw the missile go home. The rock ape fell for the third time.

When one of those taloned paws began to move again, Nymani broke. He ran, his screams echoing thinly in the air, as the thing lurched up, the gory mess of its head weaving about. If his feet would have obeyed him, Dane might have followed the Khatkan. As it was, he drew his ray and aimed it at that shambling thing. Tau struck up the barrel.

The medic's face was livid; there was the same horror in his eyes. But he moved out to front that monster.

A spot of shadow coalesced on the ground, deepened in hue, took on substance. Crouched low facing the rock ape, its haunches quivering for a deadly spring, narrowed green eyes holding on its prey, was a black leopard.

The tiny forward and backward movements of its body steadied, and it arched through the air, brought down the ape. A pitting, snarling tangle rolled across the slope—and was gone!

Asaki's hands shook as he drew them down his sweating face. Jellico readied a second clip in the needler mechanically. But Tau was swaying so that Dane leaped to take the shock of the other's weight as he collapsed. Only for a moment did the medic hang so; then he struggled to stand erect.

"Magic?" Jellico's voice, as controlled as ever, broke the silence.

"Mass hallucination," Tau corrected him. "Very strong."

"How!" Asaki swallowed and began again. "How was it done?"

The medic shook his head. "Not by the usual methods, that is certain. And it worked on us—on me—when we weren't conditioned. I don't understand that!"

Dane could hardly believe it yet. He watched Jellico stride to where the tangle of struggling beasts had rolled, saw him examine bare ground on which no trace of the fight remained. They must accept Tau's explanation; it was the only sane one.

Asaki's features were suddenly convulsed with a rage so stark that Dane realized how much a veneer was the painfully built civilization of Khatka.

Lumbrilo! The Chief Ranger made of that name a curse. Then with a visible effort he controlled his emotions and came to Tau, looming over the slighter medic almost menacingly.

"How?" he demanded for the second time.

"I don't know."

"He will try again?"

"Not the same perhaps—"

But Asaki had already grasped the situation, was looking ahead.

"We shall not know," he breathed, "what is real, what is not."

"There is also this," Tau warned. "The unreal can kill the believer just as quickly as the real!"

"That I know also. It has happened too many times lately. If we could only find out how! Here are no drums, no singing —none of the tricks to tangle a man's mind that he usually uses to summon his demons. So without Lumbrilo, without his witch tools, how does he make us see what is not?"

"That we must discover and speedily, sir. Or else we shaall be lost among the unreal and the real."

"You also have the power. You can save us!" Asaki protested.

Tau drew his arm across his face. Very little of the normal color had returned to his thin, mobile features. He still leaned against Dane's supporting arm.

"A man can do only so much, sir. To battle Lumbrilo on his own ground is exhausting and I can not fight so very often."

"But will he not also be exhausted?"

"I wonder . . ." Tau gazed beyond the Khatkan to the barren ground where leopard and rock ape had ceased to be. "This magic is a tricky thing, sir. It builds and feeds upon a man's own imagination and inner fears. Lumbrilo, having triggered ours, need not strive at all, but let us ourselves raise that which will attack us."

"Drugs?" demanded Jellico.

Tau gave a start sufficient to take him out of Dane's loose hold. His hand went to the packet of aid supplies which was his own care, his eyes round with wonder and then shrewdly alert.

"Captain, we disinfected those thorn punctures of yours. Thorson, your foot salve. . . . But, no, I didn't use anything—"

"You forget, Craig, we all had scratches after that fight with the apes."

Tau sat down on the ground. With feverish haste he unsealed his medical supplies, laid out some containers. Then delicately he opened each, examined its contents closely by eye, by smell, and two by taste. When he was done he shook his head.

"If these have been in any way meddled with, I would need laboratory analysis to detect it. And I don't believe that Lumbrilo could hide traces of his work so cleverly. Or has he been off-planet? Had much to do with off-worlders?" he asked the Chief Ranger.

"By the nature of his position he is forbidden to space voyage, to have any close relationship with any off-worlder. I do not think, medic, he would choose your healing substances for his mischief. There would only be chance to aid him then in producing the effects he wants. Though there is often call for first aid in travel, he could not be *certain* you would use any of your drugs on this trip to the preserve."

"And Lumbrilo *was* certain. He threatened something such as this," Jellico reminded them.

"So it would be something which we would all use, which we had to depend upon. . . ."

"The water!" Dane had been holding his own canteen ready to drink. But as that possible explanation dawned in his mind, he smelled instead of tasted the liquid sloshing inside. There was no odor he could detect. But he remembered Tau commenting on the powdered purifier pills at their first camp.

"That's it!" Tau dug further into his kit, brought out the vial of white powder with its grainy lumps. Pouring a little into the palm of his hand he smelled it, touched it with the tip of his tongue. "Purifier and something else," he reported. "It could be one of half a dozen drugs, or some native stuff from here which we've never classified."

"True. There are drugs we have found here." Asaki scowled down at the green mat of jungle. "So our water is poisoned?"

"Do you always purify it?" Tau asked the Chief Ranger. "Surely during the centuries since your ancestors landed on Khatka you must have adapted to native water. You couldn't have lived otherwise. We must use the purifier, but must you?"

"There is water and water." Asaki shook his own canteen, his scowl growing fiercer as the gurgle from its depths was heard. "From springs on the other side of the mountains we drink—yes. But over here this close to the Mygra swamps, we have not done so. We may have to chance it."

"Do you think we are literally poisoned?" Jellico bored directly to the heart of their private fears.

"None of us have been drinking too heavily," Tau observed thoughtfully. "And I don't believe Lumbrilo had outright killing in mind. How long the effect will last I have no way of telling."

"If we saw one rock ape," Dane wondered, "why didn't we see others? And why here and now?"

"That!" Tau pointed ahead on the trail Asaki had picked for their ascent. For a long moment Dane could see nothing of any interest there and then he located it—a finger of rock. It did not point directly skyward this time, in fact it slanted so that its tip indicated their back trail. Yet in outline the spire was very similar to that outcrop from which the real rock ape had charged them the day before.

Asaki exclaimed in his own tongue and slapped his hand hard against the stock of the needler.

"We saw that and so again we saw an ape also! Had earlier we been charged by graz or jumped by a lion in such a place, then again we would have been faced by graz or lion here!"

Captain Jellico gave a bark of laughter colored only by the most sardonic humor. "Clever enough. He merely leaves it to us to select our own ghost and then repeat the performance in the next proper setting. I wonder how many rocks shaped like that one there are in these mountains? And how long will a rock ape continue to pop out from behind each one we do find?"

"Who knows? But as long as we drink this water we're going to continue to have trouble; I feel safe in promising that," Tau replied. He put the vial of doctored purifier into a separate pocket of his medical kit. "It may be a problem of how long we can go without water."

"Perhaps," Asaki said softly. "Only not all the water on Khatka comes running in streams."

"Fruit?" Tau asked.

"No, trees. Lumbrilo is not a hunter, nor could he be certain when and where his magic would go to work. Unless the flitter was deliberately sabotaged, he was planning for us to use our canteens in the preserve. That is lion country and there are long distances between springs. This is jungle below us and there is a source there I think we can safely tap. But first I must find Nymani and prove to him that this is truly deviltry of a sort, but not demon inspired."

He was gone, running lightly down-slope in the direction his hunter had taken, and Dane spoke to Captain Jellico.

"What's this about water in trees, sir?"

"There is a species of tree here, not too common, with a thickened trunk. It stores water during the rainy season to live on in the hot months. Since we are in the transition period between rains, we could tap it—if we locate one of the trees. How about that, Tau? Dare we drink that without a purifier?"

"Probably a choice of two evils, sir. But we have had our preventive shots. Personally, I'd rather battle disease than take a chance on a mind-twisting drug. You can go without water just so long. . . ."

"I'd like to have a little talk with Lumbrilo," remarked Jellico, the mildness in his voice very deceptive.

"I'm *going* to have a little talk with Lumbrilo, if and when we see him again!" promised Tau.

"What are our chances, sir?" Dane asked. He screwed the cap back on his canteen, his mouth feeling twice as dry since he knew he dared not drink.

"Well, we've faced gambles before." Tau sealed the medical kit. "I'd like to see one of those trees before sundown. And I don't want to face another pointed rock today!"

"Why the leopard?" asked Jellico reflectively. "Another case of using flame to fight fire? But Lumbrilo wasn't among those present to be impressed."

Tau rubbed his hand across his forehead. "I don't really know, sir. Maybe I could have made the ape vanish without a counter projection, but I don't think so. With these hallucinations it is better to battle one vision against another for the benefit of those involved. And I can't even tell you why I selected a leopard—it just flashed into mind as about the fastest and most deadly animal fighter I could recall at that moment."

"You'd better work out a good list of such fighters." Jellico's grim humor showed again. "I can supply a few if you need them. Not that I don't share your hope we won't see any more trigger rocks. Here comes Asaki with his wandering boy."

The Chief Ranger was half-leading, half-supporting his hunter, and Nymani seemed only half-conscious. Tau got to his feet and hurried to meet them. It would appear that their search for the water tree would be delayed.

VI

THEY WITHDREW to a spot hacked from the edge of the jungle, leaving a screen of green between them and the traitorous up-slope. But within the few hours of daylight left them, it was proven that Asaki had been overly optimistic in his hopes of discovering a water tree. They were now in a narrow tongue of land between the range and the swamps, and this territory was limited. Nymani, still shaken, was of little help, and the spacemen did not dare to strike out into unexplored land alone.

So they mouthed dry concentrates and dared not drink. Dane was tempted to pour out the liquid in his canteen. Water so close to hand was a continual torment. And, now that they were away from the heights and the possibility of more finger-shaped rocks, surely the threat in that moisture was small in comparison to the needs of his body. Only that caution which was drilled into every Free Trader supplied a brake to his thirst.

Jellico drew the back of his hand across cracked lips. "Suppose we should draw lots—some of us drink, one or two not. Could we manage that way until we were over the mountains?"

"I wouldn't want to chance it, unless we are left with no other choice. There is no way of telling how long the drug works. Frankly right now I'm not even sure I could detect a hallucination for very long under these conditions," was Tau's discouraging verdict.

If any of them slept that night, they did so only in snatches. The apprehension which had come with the previous night was back, intensified, and that lurking, indefinable fear rode them hard.

They were shaken out of their private terrors shortly after dawn. There were always sounds to be heard in the jungle: the cries of unseen birds, the crash of some tree eaten alive by parasitic sapping. But what broke now was no bird call, no isolated tree falling. A trumpeting roar, the crackling smash of vegetation, heralded a real menace. Asaki spun to face northward, though there was nothing to be seen there except the unshaken wall of the jungle.

"Graz! Graz on stampede!" Nymani joined his superior.

Jellico arose swiftly and Dane read on the captain's face the seriousness of this. The off-worlder turned to his own men with a sharp order. "On your feet! We may have to move on the double. Up-mountain?" he demanded of the Chief Ranger.

The other was still listening, not only with his ears but with the whole of his tense body. Three of the deer-like creatures they had hunted for food broke out of the green wall, fled past the men as if the latter was invisible. And behind them, the hunted now and not the hunter, came a lion, its strikingly marked black-and-white hide dramatic in the light of the morning. It showed fangs in a snarl and then was gone in one huge bound. More deer things, scurrying of other small creatures, moving too fast for clear identification, and behind them the fury of destruction which marked the headlong advance of Khatka's largest mammals slamming through the jungle.

They had started up-slope when Nymani cried out. A white bulk, hard to distinguish in that light against the gray of the earth, headed after them. Dane had a fleeting glimpse of curled tusks, of an open moth, raw-red and wide enough to engulf his whole head, of shaggy legs driving at an unbelievable pace. Asaki snapped a beam from the needler. The white monster roared and came on. They dived for the scant cover offered as the graz bull died, not two yards away from the Chief Ranger, its heavy body skidding along the earth with the force of its speed as it went down.

"That did it!" Jellico sighted coolly with his blaster as a second bull, fighting mad, tore from the jungle and pounded at them. Behind it a third tusked head thrust out of the brush; large eyes searched for an enemy. Dane studied the dead bull, but the animal did not come to life this time. These were not hallucinations. And the malignancy of the

137

rock apes, the cunning of the native Khatkan lion, were pallid things compared to a graz herd on the rampage.

The second bull yelped with an almost canine complaint as Jellico's blaster caught it head-on. Blinded, the beast blundered ahead, climbing the mountain side. The third met a ray from Nymani's needler. But the Chief Ranger leaped from behind his sheltering rock to the one where the captain had taken refuge and pulled him into the open.

"They must not corner us here!"

Jellico agreed to that. "Come on!" he barked to Tau and Dane.

They fled along a rough way, trying to gain altitude, but finding a rising cliff wall which could not be easily climbed. Two more graz went down, one badly wounded, one safely dead. Behind them more white heads came from the brush. What original cause had started the stampede the fugitives could not guess, but now the fear and anger of the animals were centering upon them.

And, in spite of their efforts, the party was being herded into a pocket between the jungle below, where the main body of graz crashed along, and a steep wall. Given time to find the necessary finger and toe holds, a man might climb that wall, but they could not attempt it now. The portion of ledge on which they ran, stopped to fire, and then ran on again, angled to the southeast. And so they came to its end quickly, a drop ending in a plain of yellow-gray mud studded with clumps of bleached vegetation which led, like steppingstones, toward a tangle of matted, sickly looking plants and reeds.

"All right"—Tau faced around—"what do we do now? Space lift? And using what for wings or jets?"

As if the graz could sense that they now had their victims safely cornered, what must have been a goodly segment of the herd hooked their way from the jungle and started up. Puffing, digging in those sturdy legs which had to take the massive weight of their barrel-shaped bodies, they made their way determinedly up-grade. One might almost believe that they had intelligently planned this end for their drive.

"We go down!" Asaki yelled, and used his needler on the leader of that climbing platoon.

"The brush islands," Nymani amended. "I show you!" He thrust his needler at Jellico and was over the edge of the ledge, hanging by his hands and swinging his weight back and forth like a pendulum. At the up-swing of his body to the right, he let go and plunged out, landing half across one of the reed islets. The Khatkan clawed his way to his knees, gained his feet, and leaped for the next bit of solid ground.

"You, Thorson!" Jellico jerked his head at Dane and the younger spaceman holstered his fire ray, slipped gingerly over the drop and prepared to repeat Nymani's feat as best he could.

He was not quite as successful with his sidewise swing, landing with only his forearms across the islet, the rest of his body being swiftly embedded in what was ooze covered only with a thin crust of dried matter. The stench of the stuff was sickening, but the fear of being entrapped in it gave him the necessary impetus to push forward, though what was meant to be a swift half-dive was more of a worm's progress. He grabbed frantically at brittle stems, at coarse grass which cut like knives at his hands. But some of the material held and he lay face down on a lump which did not give under his weight.

There was no time to linger; he had to get to the next patch, to free this dubious landing place for the men embattled on the rise above. Stumbling up, Dane judged the distance with a space-trained eye and jumped to a knob Nymani had already quitted. The Khatkan was more than halfway along toward that promise of solid ground which the tangled mass of leprous vegetation led to, zigzagging expertly from islet to islet.

There was a crash and a roar behind. Dane balanced on the third of the minute islands to look back. He saw the lash of blaster fire on the top of the cliff, Tau on his knees on the first of their chain of steppingstones, and a graz sprawled head and forequarters in the sucking muck where it had dived past the two defenders above. Needler and blaster fired together again, and then Jellico swung over the cliff rim. Tau waved vigorously and Dane took off for the next islet, just making it by lucky chance.

The rest of the journey he took in a rush, trying not to think of anything but the necessity of landing on some spot of firm ground. His last leap of all was too short, so that he went knee deep in a particularly evil-smelling pool where yellow scum spattered his breeches and he experienced the insidious pull of the bottomless stuff. A stout branch whipped across his shoulder and he caught it. With Nymani's wiry strength on the other end, Dane worked free and sat, white-faced and shivering, on a mat of brush, while the Khatkan hunter turned his attention to the safety of Tau, the next arrival.

More fortunate, or more skillfull than Dane, the medic made the hop from the last tuft without mishap. But he was blowing heavily as he collapsed beside the other spaceman. Together they watched the progress of their captain.

Safe on the second tussock from the shore, Jellico halted, edged carefully around and used the needler Nymani had left with him. A shaggy head tossed and the bull fronting Asaki on the cliff went down. The Chief Ranger dodged quickly to the right and a second beast rushed out and over, to join its mired comrade in the swamp below. As Jellico shot again, the Khatkan slung his needler and went over to gain the first islet.

One more graz was wounded but luckily it hunched about, turning its formidable tusks on those that followed, thus keeping the path clear for its enemies. Jellico was making the journey, sure-footedly, with the Chief Ranger only one hillock behind. Tau sighed.

"Someday maybe this will be just another tall tale and we'll all be thought liars when we spout it," he observed. "That is if we survive to tell it. So now which way do we go? If I had my choice it would be up!"

When Dane pulled himself to his feet and surveyed their small refuge, he was ready to agree to that. For the space, packed with dead and dying vegetable matter until one sank calf deep, was a triangle with a narrow point running east into the swamp.

"They don't give up easily, do they?" Jellico looked back to the shore and the cliff. Though the wounded graz bull still held the heights against its fellows, there were others breaking from the jungle on the lower level, wandering back and forth to paw the earth, rip up soil with their tusks, and otherwise threaten anyone who would try to return to the strip they patrolled.

"They will not," Asaki answered bleakly. "Arouse a graz and it will trail you for days; kill any of the herd and you have little hope of escaping them on foot."

It would seem now that the swamp was a deterrent to pursuit. The two beasts that had fallen in the mire moaned in a pitiful rising note. They had ceased to struggle and several of their kind clustered on the shore near them, calling entreatingly. Asaki took careful aim with the needler and put one animal after another out of its misery. But the flash of those shots angered those on shore to a higher pitch of rage.

"No going back," he said. "At least not for several days."

Tau slapped a black, four-winged insect which had settled on his arm, its jaws wide open for a sampling bite. "We can't very well perch here until they forget all about us," he pointed out. "Not without water we can trust, and with the local wild life ready to test us for tasty eating."

Nymani had prowled along the swampward point of their island, and now he made his report.

"There is more high land to the east. Perhaps it will give us a bridge across."

At that moment Dane doubted his ability to make any more leaps from island to island. And it would seem Tau shared his discouragement.

"I don't suppose you could discourage our friends on shore there with a few more shots?"

Asaki shook his head. "We do not have clips enough to settle a whole herd. These might retreat from sight but they would be waiting for us in the bush, and that would mean certain death. We shall have to take the swamp road."

If Dane had considered their earlier march misery, this was sheer torture. Since footing was never secure, falls were frequent, and within a quarter-hour they were all plastered with evil-smelling slime and mud which hardened to rock consistency when exposed to the air. Painful as this was, it did protect a portion of their bodies from the insects with which the swamp was well stocked.

And, in spite of their efforts to find a way out, the only possible paths led them deeper into the center of the unexplored morass. At last Asaki called a halt and a council to consider retreat. To locate an island from which they could at least watch the shore appealed very strongly indeed.

"We have to have water." Tau's voice was a harsh croak, issuing out of a mask of green mud festooned with trailing weeds.

"This ground is rising." Asaki smacked the stock of his

needler against the surface on which he crouched. "I think perhaps there may be clean land soon to come."

Jellico hitched his way up a sapling, now bending under his weight. Through the vision lenses he studied the route ahead.

"You're right about that," he called to the Chief Ranger. "There's a showing of the right sort of green to the left, about half a mile on. And," he glanced about at the westering sun, "we have about an hour yet of good light in which to make it. I wouldn't try such a run after dark."

That promise of green bolstered their weary spirits for a last exhausting effort. Once again they were faced with a series of islet leaps, and now they carried with them brush culled from the bigger tussocks to aid in times of need.

When Dane scrambled up the last pull, staggered, and went down to his knees again, he knew he was done. He did not even move at an excited cry from Nymani, echoed a moment later by Asaki. It was not until the latter leaned over him, a canteen open in his hand, that Dane aroused a little.

"Drink!" the Khatkan urged. "We have found a water tree. This is fresh."

The liquid might have been fresh, but it also had a peculiar taste, which Dane did not note until he had gulped down a generous swallow. At that moment he was past caring about anything but the fact that he did have a portion of drinkable stuff in hand.

Here the stunted, unnatural growth of the swamplands had given away to the more normal vegetation of the jungle-clad lowlands. Had they come clear across the swamp, Dane wondered dully, or was this only a large island in the midst of the stinking boglands?

He drank again and regained strength enough to crawl to where his shipmates lay. It was some time before he was interested in much besides the fact that he could drink when he wished. Then he watched Jellico waver to his feet, his head turned eastward. Tau, too, sat up as if alerted by the *Queen's* alarm buzzer.

The Khatkans were gone, perhaps back to the water tree. But all three of the spacemen heard that sound, a far off throbbing rhythm which was a vibration as well. Jellico looked to Tau.

"Drums?"

"Could be." The medic screwed the cap back on his canteen. "I'd say we have company—only I'd like to know what kind!"

They might have been mistaken about the drums, but none of them could have been mistaken about the bolt which came out of nowhere to slice through a tree trunk as a knife might slash wet clay. Blaster—and a particular type of blaster!

"Patrol issue!" Tau lay flat, squeezing himself against the earth as if he wished he could ooze into it.

Jellico wriggled toward the bush in answer to a low call from Asaki, and the others made a worm's progress in his wake. Under cover they found the Chief Ranger reading his needler.

"Poacher camp here," he explained bleakly. "And they know about us."

"A perfect end to a stinking day," remarked Tau dispassionately. "We might have guessed something of this sort was waiting." He tried to rub away some of the dried clay coating his chin. "But do poachers use drums?"

The Chief Ranger scowled. "That is what Nymani has gone to find out."

VII

DARKNESS CLOSED in while they waited for Nymani's return. There had been no further attack from the blaster wielder; perhaps he was only trying to pin them down where they were. Out over the swamp, weird patches of phosphorescence moved in small ghostly clouds, and bright dots of insects with their own built-in lighting systems flashed spark-fashion or sailed serenely on regular flight plans. At night the wonder of the place was far removed from the squalid reality of the day. They chewed on their rations, drank sparingly of the water, and tried to keep alert to any sight or sound.

That monotonous undertone, which might or might not be drums, continued as a basic hum to the noises of the night, drowned out at intervals by a splash, a mutter or cry from some swamp creature. Beside Dane, Jellico stiffened, moved his blaster, as someone wriggled through the brush, trilling softly.

"Off-worlders," Nymani reported in gasps to Asaki, "and outlaws, too. They make a hunting sing—tomorrow they march for a killing."

Asaki rested his chin on his broad forearm. "Outlaws?"

"They show no lord's badge. But each I saw wears a bracelet of three, five, or ten tails. They are Trackers indeed, and Hunters of the best!"

"They have huts?"

"Not so. There are no dwellers in the inners courts here." Out of habit Nymani used the polite term for the women of his race. "I would say they tarry only for the space of a hunt. And on the boots of one I saw salt crust."

"Salt crust!" Asaki snapped and half arose. "So that is the type of lure they use. There must be a saline mire near here to pull game—"

"How many off-worlders?" Jellico broke in.

"Three who are Hunters, one who is different."

"How different?" questioned Asaki.

"He wears upon his body garments which are strange; on his head a round covering such as we see upon the off-worlders of the ships—"

"A spaceman!"

Asaki laughed harshly. "Why not? They must have some method of transporting their hides."

"You can't tell me," Jellico returned, "that anyone is able to set a ship down in this muck. It would simply be buried for all time."

"But, Captain, what type of a spaceport does a Free Trader need? Do you not planet your own ship on worlds where there are no waiting cradles, no fitter shops, none of the conveniences such as mark the field Combine maintains on Xecho?"

"Of course I do. But one does need a reasonably smooth stretch of territory, open enough so the tail flames won't start a forest fire. You don't ever ride a tail push down in a swamp!"

"Which testifies to a trail out of here, fairly well-traveled, and some kind of a usable landing space not too far away," Asaki replied. "And that could very well serve us."

"But they know we are here," Tau pointed out.

It was Nymani's turn to laugh. "Man from the stars, there is no trail so well-hidden that a Ranger of the preserves cannot nose it out, nor any Hunter—be he a two or five bracelet veteran—who can keep pinned down a determined man of the forest service!"

Dane lost interest in the argument at that moment. He was at the edge of their line, the nearest to the swamp, and he had been watching patches of ghostly light flitting above the rank water-weeds. For the past few moments those wisps of faded radiance had been gathering into a growing anthropomorphic blot hanging over the morass several yards away. And the misty outlines were now assuming more concrete shape. He watched, unable to believe in what he was seeing At first the general outline, non-defined as it was, made him think of a rock ape. But there were no pointed ears above the round skull, no snout on the visage turned in profile toward him.

More and more patches of swamp luminescence were drawn to that glowing figure. What balanced there now, as if walking the treacherous surface of the swampland, was no animal. It was a man, or the semblance of one, a small, thin man—a man he had seen once before, on the terrace of Asaki's mountain fortress.

The thing stood almost complete, its head cocked in what was an attitude of listening.

"Lumbrilo!" Dane identified it, still knowing that the witch doctor could not be standing there listening for them. But, to shake him still farther, the head turned at his cry. Only there were no eyes, no features on the white expanse which should have been a face. And somehow that made the monster more menacing, convincing Dane against sane logic that the thing *was* spying on them.

"Demon!" That was Nymani; and over his sudden quaver, robbed of all the confidence which had been there only moments earlier, came Asaki's demand:

"What stands there, Medic? Tell us that!"

"A whip to drive us out of hiding, sir. As you know as well as I. If Nymani spied upon them, then they have spied upon us in turn. And this, I think, also answers another question. If there is a canker of trouble on Khatka, then Lumbrilo is close to its root."

"Nymani!" The Chief Ranger's voice was the crack of a lash. "Will you forget again that you are a man, and run crying for shelter against a shaft of light? As this off-world Medic says, Lumbrilo fashions such as that to drive us into our enemies' hands!"

The shadow thing in the swamp moved, putting its foot forward on surface which would not bear the weight of a human body, taking a deliberate step and then another, heading for the concealing brush where the fugitives lay.

"Can you get rid of it, Tau?" Jellico asked in his usual crisp voice. He might have been inquiring about some problem aboard the *Queen*.

"I'd rather get at the source." There was a grim note in the Medic's reply. "And to do that I want to look at their camp."

"Well enough!" Asaki crept back in the brush.

The ghost of that which was not a man had reached the shore of the island, stood there, its blank head turned toward them. Weird as it was, now that the first shock of sighting it was over, the spacemen could accept and dismiss it as they had not been so able to dismiss the phantom rock ape.

"If that thing was sent to drive us," Dane ventured, "wouldn't we be playing their game by going inland now?"

The Chief Ranger did not pause in his crawl to the left. "I think not. They do not expect us to arrive with our wits about us. Panic-stricken men are easy to pull down. This time Lumbrilo has overreached himself. Had he not played that game with the rock ape, he might have been able to stampede us now."

Though the white thing continued to move inland, it did not change course to fall in behind them on the new route. Whatever it was, it did not possess a mind.

There was a rustling, faint but distinguishable. Then Dane caught Nymani's whisper.

"The one left to watch the inland trail does so no longer. We need not fear an alarm from *him*. Also, here is another blaster for our use."

Away from the open by the swamp, the gloom was deeper. Dane was guided only by the noises that the less-experienced Jellico and Tau made in their progress.

They edged down into a small cut, floored with reeds and mud, where some of the moisture from the soggy land about them gathered into a half pool. Straight through this swale the Khatkans set course.

The drum beat grew louder. Now there was a glow against the dark—fire ahead? Dane squirmed forward and at last gained a vantage point from which to survey the poachers' camp.

There were shelters erected there, three of them, but they were mainly roofs of leaves and branches. In two of them were stored bales of hides sewn into plastic cloth, ready to ship. Before the third hut lounged four off-worlders. And Nymani was very right; one of them wore ship's uniform.

To the right of the fire was a ring of natives and another man, slightly apart, who beat the drum. But of the witch doctor there was no sign. And Dane, thinking of that mist-born thing at the swamp's edge, shivered. He could believe Tau's explanation of the drug which produced hallucinations back on the mountain side. But how that likeness fashioned of phosphorescence had been sent by an absent man to hunt his enemies was a eerie puzzle.

"Lumbrilo is not here." Nymani's thoughts must have been moving along the same path.

Dane could hear movements in the dark beside him.

"There's a long-distance com unit in that third hut," Tau observed.

"So I see," Jellico snapped. "Could you reach your men over the mountain with that, sir?"

"I do not know. But if Lumbrilo is not here, how can he make his image walk the night?" the Chief Ranger demanded impatiently.

"We shall see. If Lumbrilo is not here—he shall come." And the promise in Tau's tone was sure. "Those off-worlders will have to be out of action first. And with that walking thing sent to drive us in, they must be waiting for us."

"If they have sentries out, I will silence them!" promised Nymani.

"You have a plan?" Asaki's wide shoulders and upheld head showed for an instant against the light from the camp.

"You want Lumbrilo," Tau replied. "Very well, sir, I believe I can give him to you, and in the doing discredit him with your Khatkans. But not with the off-worlders free to move."

The program was not going to be easy, Dane decided. Every one of the poachers was armed with a Patrol blaster of the latest type, and a small part of his mind speculated as to what would be the result of that information conveyed to official quarters. Free Traders and Patrolmen did not always see eye-to-eye over the proper action to be taken on the galactic frontier. The *Queen's* crew had had one such brush with authority in the immediate past. But each realized that the other had an important role in the general scheme of things, and if it came to a clash between the law and outlaws, Free Traders fought beside the Patrol.

"Why not give them what they expect—with reservations?" inquired Jellico. "They've set us up to be stampeded into camp, flying ahead of that tame ghost of theirs. Suppose we do stampede—after Nymani has removed any sentries—stampede so well we sweep right over them? I want to get at that com unit."

"You don't think they'll just mow us down as we come in?"

"You delivered a blow to Lumbrilo's pride; he won't be satisfied with just your burning," the captain answered Tau, "not if I'm any judge of character. And we'd furnish hostages of a sort—especially the Chief Ranger. No, if they had wanted to kill us they would have shot us off those islands when we came here. There would have been no playing around with ghosts and goblins."

"There is reason in your words. And it is true they would like to have me, those outlaws down there," Asaki commented. "I am of the Magawaya and we have pressed always for stronger security methods to be used against such as they. But I do not see how we can take the camp."

"We won't go in from the front—as they expect us to do. But a try from the north, getting at the off-worlders first. . . . Three men causing enough disturbance to cover operations of the other two. . . ."

"So?" There was a moment of silence as the Chief Ranger evaluated that. Then he added a few comments of his own.

"That off-worlder who wears spaceman's clothing, his weapon is not drawn, though the others are ready. But I believe that you are right in thinking they expect to be warned by sentries. Those we can see to. Suppose then, Captain, you and I play the fear-crazed men running from demons. Nymani will cover us from the dark and your two men—"

Tau spoke up, "Give me leave to flush out our other quarry, sir. I believe I can keep him occupied. Dane, you'll take the drum."

"Drum?" With his mind on blasters, it was startling to be offered a noise-maker.

"It's your business to get that drum. And when you get it I want you to beat out 'Terra Bound.' You certainly can play that, can't you?"

"I don't understand," Dane began and then swallowed the rest of his protest, knowing that Tau was not going to explain why he needed to have the hackneyed popular song of the spaceways played in a Khatkan swamp. As a Free Trader he had had quite a few odd jobs handed him during the past couple of years, but this was the first time he had been ordered to serve as a musician.

They waited for Nymani through dragging minutes. Surely those in the camp would expect their arrival soon now? Dane's fire ray was in his hand as he measured the distance to the drummer's stand.

"It is done," Nymani whispered from the darkness behind them. Jellico and the Chief Ranger moved to the left; Tau crept to the right and Dane pushed level with the medic.

"When they move"—Tau's lips were beside his ear—"jump for that drum. I don't care how you get it, but get it and keep it!"

"Yes, sir!"

There was a wailing cry from the north, a howl of witless fear. The singers stopped in mid-note, the drummer paused, his hand uplifted. Dane darted forward in a plunge which carried him to that man. The Khatkan did not have time to rise from his knees as the barrel of the fire rod struck his head, sending him spinning. Then the drum was cradled in the spaceman's arm, close to his chest, his weapon aimed across it at the startled natives.

The crackle of blaster fire, the shrill whine of needlers in action, raised a bedlam from the other end of the camp. Backing up a little, Dane went down on one knee, his weapon ready to sweep over the bewildered natives, the drum resting on the earth against his body. Keeping the fire rod steady, his left hand went to work, not in the muted cadence the Khatkan drummer had chosen, but in hard and vigorous thumps which rolled across the clamor of the fight. There was no forgetting the beat of "Terra Bound" and he delivered it with force, so that the familiar da-dah-da-da droned loud enough to awaken the whole camp.

Dane's move appeared to completely baffle the Khatkan outlaws. They stared at him, the whites of their eyes doubly noticeable in their dark faces, their mouths a little agape. As usual the unexpected had driven them off guard. He dared not look away from that gathering to see how the fight at the other end of the camp was progressing. But he did see Tau's advance.

The medic came into the light of the fire, not with his ordinary loose-limbed spaceman's stride, but mincingly, with a dancing step, and he was singing to the drum beat of "Terra Bound." Dane could not understand the words, but he knew that they patterned in and out of the drum beats, weaving a net between singer and listeners as Lumbrilo had woven his net on the mountain terrace.

Tau had them! Had every one of the native outlaws ensnared, so that Dane rested his weapon across his knee and took up the lower beat with the fingers of his right hand as well.

Da-dah-da-da . . . The innocuous repetitive refrain of the original song which had been repeating itself in his mind faded, and somehow he caught the menace in the new words Tau was mouthing.

Twice the medic shuffled about a circle of his own making. Then he stooped, took a hunting knife from the belt of the nearest Khatkan and held it point out toward the dark east. Dane would not have believed the medic knew the drill he now displayed, for with no opponent save the dancing firelight he fought a knife duel, feinting, striking, twisting, retreating, attacking, all in time to the beat of the drum Dane was no longer conscious of playing. And as he strove it was very easy to picture another fighting against him. So that when the knife came up in a vicious thrust which was the finish of this last attack, Dane stared stupidly at the ground, half expecting to see a body lying there.

Once more Tau ceremoniously saluted with his blade to the east. The he laid it on the ground and stood astride its gleaming length.

"Lumbrilo!" His confident voice arose above the call of the drum. "Lumbrilo—I am waiting."

VIII

VAGUELY AWARE that the clamor at the other end of the camp had died away, Dane muted the sound of his drum. Over its round top he could watch the Khatkan outlaws; their heads bobbed and swayed in time to the beat of his fingers. He, too, could feel the pull of Tau's voice. But what would come in answer? That shadowy thing which had been loosed to drive them here? Or the man himself?

To Dane, the ruddy light of the fire dimmed, yet there was no actual dying of those flames which coiled and thrust around the wood. And the acrid scent of burning was thick. How much of what followed was real, how much the product of his tense nerves, Dane was never afterwards able to tell. In fact, whether all the witnesses there saw the same sights could be questioned. Did each man, Khatkan and off-worlder, see only what his particular set of emotions and memories dictated?

Something swept in from the east, something which was not as tangible as the creature born of swamp mist. Rather it came as an unseen menace to the fire, and all that fire signifies to human kind—security, comradeship, a weapon against the age-old forces of the dangerous night. Was that threat, too, only in their minds? Or had Lumbrilo some power to so shape his hatred?

The unseen was cold; it sapped a man's strength, bit at his brain, weighted his hands and feet, weakened him. It strove to soften him into clay another could remold. Nothingness, darkness, all that was opposed to life and warmth and reality, arose in the night, gathered together against them.

Yet still Tau fronted that invisible wave, his head high. And between his sturdily planted feet the knife gleamed bright with a radiance of its own.

"Ahhh—" Tau's voice curled out, to pierce that creeping menace. Then he was singing again, the cadence of his unknown words rising a little above the pattern wrought by the drum.

Dane forced his heavy hands to continue the beat, his wrists to rise and fall in defiance of that which crept to eat their strength and make them less than men.

"Lumbrilo! I, Tau, of another star, another sky, another world, bid you come forth and range your power against mine!" Now there was a sharper note in that demand, the snap of an order.

He was answered by another wave of the black negation—stronger, rolling up to smash them down, as a wave in the heavy surf of a wild ocean pounds its force against the beach. This time Dane thought he could see that dark mass. He tore his eyes away before it took on substance, concentrating on the movements of his hands against the drum head, refusing to believe that hammer of power was rising to flatten them all. He had heard Tau describe such things in the past. But told in familiar quarters on board the *Queen*, such experiences were only stories. Here was danger unleashed. Yet the medic stood unbowed as the wave broke upon him in full.

And, advancing under the crest of that lick of destruction, came its controller. This was no ghost drawn from the materials of the swamp; this was a man, walking quietly, his hands as empty as Tau's, yet grasping weapons none of them could see.

In the firelight, as the wave receded sullenly, men moaned, lay face down upon the ground, beat their hands feebly against the earth. But, as Lumbrilo came on from the shadows, one of them got to his hands and knees, moving with small tortured jerks. He crawled toward Tau, his head lolling on his shoulders as the head of the dead rock ape had done. Dane patted the drum with one hand while, with the other, he groped for his fire ray. He tried to shout in warning and found that he could not utter a sound.

Tau's arm moved, raised from his side, made a circling motion.

The creeping man, his eyes rolled up in his head until only the whites gleamed blindly in the limited light, followed that gesture. He drew level with the medic, passed beyond toward Lumbrilo, whining as a hound prevented from obeying his master night lament.

"So be it, Lumbrilo," Tau said. "This is between you and me. Or do you not dare to risk your power against mine? Is Lumbrilo so weak a one that he must send another to do his will?"

Raising both hands again the medic brought them down, curling inward, until he stooped and touched them to the ground. When he straightened once again the knife was in his grasp and he tossed it behind him.

The smoke from the fire swirled out in a long tongue, coiled about Lumbrilo and was gone. A black and white beast stood where the man had been, its tufted tail lashing, its muzzle a mask of snarling hate and blood lust.

But Tau met that transformation with laughter which was like the lash of a whip.

"We both be men, you and I, Lumbrilo. Meet me as a man and keep those trickeries for those who have not the clear sight. A child plays as a child, so—" Tau's voice came in a rumble, but Tau was gone. The huge, hairy thing which swayed in his place turned a gorilla's beast visage to his enemy. For a breathless moment Terran ape confronted Khatkan lion. Then the spaceman was himself again. "The time for games is over, man of Khatka. You have tried to hunt us to our deaths, have you not? Therefore death shall be the portion of the loser now."

Lion vanished, man stood watching, alertly, as swordsman night face swordsman with a blood feud lying on their blades. To Dane's eyes the Khatkan made no move. Yet, the fire leaped high, as if freshly fed, and flames burst from the wood, flew into the air, red and perilous birds, darting at Tau until they outlined him from the ground under his boots to an arch over his head. They united and spun faster until Dane, watching with dazzled eyes, saw the wheel become a blur of light, hiding Tau within its fiery core. His own wrists ached with the strain of his drumming as he lifted one hand and tried to shield his sight from the glare of that pillar of fire.

Lumbrilo was chanting—a heavy blatt of words. Dane stiffened; his traitorous hands were falling into the rhythm of that other song! Straightaway he raised both from the drum head, brought them down in a discordate series of thumps which bore no relation to either the song Tau wanted or that which Lumbrilo was now crooning. *Thump-thump thump*—Dane beat it out frantically, belaboring the drum head as he wanted to sink his fists home on the body of the Khatkan witch doctor.

The pillar of fire swayed, fluttered as if a wind drove it—and was gone. Tau, unmarked, smiled.

"Fire!" He pointed his fingers at Lumbrilo. "Would you try earth, and water, and air also, wizard? Call hither your whirlwind, up your flood, summon the land to quake. None of those shall bring me down!"

Shapes came flooding out of the night, some monstrous, some human, streaming past Lumbrilo to crowd into the circle of firelight. Some Dane thought he knew, some were strangers. Men wearing space uniforms, or the dress of other worlds, women—they strode, wept, mingled with the monsters to laugh, curse, threaten.

Dane guessed that Lumbrilo sent now against the Terran the harvest of the medic's own memories. He shut his eyes against this enforced intrusion upon another's past, but not before he saw Tau's face, strained, fined to the well-shaped bones beneath the thin flesh, holding still a twisted smile as he met each memory, accepted the pain it held for him, and set it aside unshaken.

"This, too, has no power any longer, man who walks in the dark."

Dane opened his eyes. Those crowding wraiths were fading, losing substance. Lumbrilo crouched, his lips drawn back from his teeth, his hatred plain to read.

"I am not clay to be molded by your hands, Lumbrilo. And now I say that the time has come to call an end—"

Tau raised his hands slowly once again, holding them away from his body, palms pointing earthward. And beneath them, on either side of the spaceman, two black shadows gathered on the surface of the ground.

"You have fettered yourself with your own bounds. As you have been the hunter, so shall you now be the hunted."

Those shadows were growing as plants might issue from

the packed soil of the camping ground. When his hands were shoulder high, Tau held them steady. Now on either side of his tautly held body crouched one of the black-and-white lions with which Lumbrilo had identified his own brand of magic throughout the year.

Lumbrilo's "lion" had been larger than life, more intelligent, more dangerous, subtly different from the normal animal it counterfeited. So now were these. And both of them raised their heads to gaze intently into the medic's face.

"Hunt well, brothers in fur," he said slowly, almost caressingly. "Him whom you hunt shall grant you sport in the going."

"Stop it!" A man leaped from the shadows behind the witch doctor. Firelight made plain his off-world dress, and he swung up a blaster, aiming at the nearest of the waiting beasts. That flash struck true, but it neither killed nor even singed the fine fur of the animal's pelt.

As the blaster's aim was swung from beast to man, Dane fired first. His ray brought a scream from the other, who dropped his weapon from a badly seared hand to reel back, cursing.

Tau waved his hands gently. The great animal heads turned obediently, until the red eyes were set on Lumbrilo. Facing them, the witch doctor straightened, spat out his hate at the medic:

"I do not run to be hunted, devil man!"

"I think you do, Lumbrilo. For you must taste fear now as you have made other men drink of it, so that it fills your blood and races through your body, clouds your mind to make of you less than a man. You have hunted out those who doubted your power, who stood in your chosen path, whom you wanted removed from the earth of Khatka. Do you doubt that they wait in the last dark for you now, ready to greet you, witch doctor? What they have known, you shall also know. This night you have shown me all that lies in my past that is weak, that was evil, that I may regret or find sorrow for. So shall you also remember through the few hours left you. Aye, you *shall* run, Lumbrilo!"

As he spoke, Tau approached the other, the two black-and-white hunters pacing beside him. Now he stooped and caught up a pinch of soil and spat upon it three times. Then he threw the tiny clod of earth at the witch doctor. It struck

Lumbrilo just above the heart and the man reeled under what might have been a murderous blow.

The Khatkan broke then, completely. With a wailing cry he whirled and ran, crashing into the brush as one who runs blindly and without hope. Behind him the two beasts leaped noiselessly together and all three were gone.

Tau swayed, put his hand to his head. Dane kicked away the drum, arose from his cramped position stiffly to go to him. But the medic was not yet done. He returned to stand over the prostrate native hunters and he clapped his hands sharply.

"You are men, and you shall act as men henceforth. That which was, is no longer. Stand free, for the dark power follows him who misused it, and fear no longer eats from your basins, drinks from your cups, or lies beside you on the sleep mats."

"Tau!" Jellico's shout reached them over the cries of the rousing Khatkans. But Dane was there first, catching the medic before he slumped to the ground; but he was dragged with that dead weight until he sat with the medic's head on his shoulder, the other's body resting heavily against him. For one horror-filled moment Dane feared that he did indeed hold a dead man, that one of the outlaw Hunters must have struck a last blow for his discredited leader. Then Tau sighed and began to breathe deeply. Dane glanced up, amazed, at the captain.

"He's asleep!"

Jellico knelt and his hand went to test heart beat, then to touch the medic's worn and dirty face. "Best thing for him," he said briskly. "He's had it."

It took some time to get the facts of their triumph sorted out. Two of the off-worlder poachers were dead. The other and the spaceman were prisoners, while Nymani rounded up in addition the man Dane had burned to save Tau. When the younger spaceman returned from making the medic comfortable in the shelter, he found Asaki and Jellico holding an impromptu court of inquiry.

The dazed native Hunters had been expertly looped together by Nymani and, a little apart from them, the off-worlders were under examination.

"An I-C man, eh?" Jellico, smoothing a mud-spattered chin with a grimed hand, regarded the latest arrival measuringly. "Trying to run in and break a Combine charter, were you? You'd better spill the facts; your own head office will disown you, you ought to know that. They never back any failures in these undercover deals."

"I want medical attention," snapped the other, cradling his seared hand to his chest. "Or do you plan to turn me over to these savages?"

"Seeing as how you tried to blast our medic," replied the captain with a grin which was close to shark-like, "he may not feel much like patching up those fingers of yours. Stick 'em in where they have no business, and they're apt to get burned. At any rate he's not going to look at 'em until he's had a chance to rest. I'll give you first aid. And while I'm working we'll talk. I-C going into the poaching trade now? That news is going to please Combine; they have no use for you boys anyway."

His answer was lurid and uninformative. But the uniform tunic the other wore could not be so easily explained away. Dane, worn out, stretched his aching length on a pile of mats and lost all interest in the argument.

Two days later they stood once more on the same terrace where Lumbrilo had wrought his magic and met his first defeat. This time no lightning played along the mountain ridges and the blaze of the sun was so bright and clear that one could hardly believe in the fantastic happenings of that swamp clearing where men had fought with weapons not made by hands. The three from the *Queen* moved away from the parapet to meet the Chief Ranger as he came down the stairs.

"A messenger has just arrived. The hunter was hunted indeed, and his going was witnessed by many—though they did not see those which hunted him. Lumbrilo is dead; he came to his end by the Great River.

Jellico started. "But that is almost fifty miles from the swamp, on this side of the mountain!"

"He was hunted and he fled—as you promised," Asaki said to Tau. "You made strong magic, off-world man."

The medic shook his head slowly. "I but turned his own methods against him. Because he believed in his power, that same power, reflected back, broke him. Had I been facing one who did not believe. . ." He shrugged. "Our first meeting set the pattern. From that moment he feared a little that I could match him, and his uncertainty pierced a hole in his armor."

"Why on earth did you want 'Terra Bound?' " burst out Dane, still seeking an explanation for that one small mystery among the others.

Tau chuckled. "In the first place, that blasted tune has haunted us all for so long that I knew its rhythm was probably the one you could keep to without hardly knowing that you were beating it out. And, in the second place, its alien pattern was a part of our particular background, to counteract Lumbrilo's native Khatkan music, which was certainly a big factor in *his* stage setting. He must have believed that we would not find out about the drugged water and so would be prepared for any fantasy he cared to produce. When they saw us coming out over the swamp they counted us easy takings. His practice had always been with Khatkans, and he judged us by their reactions to stimuli he knew well how to use. So he failed. . . ."

Asaki smiled. "Which was good for Khatka but ill for Lumbrilo and those using him to make mischief here. The poacher and the outlaw Hunters will meet with our justice, which I do not believe they will relish. But the other two, the spaceman and the company agent, are to be sent to Xecho to face Combine authorities. It is my thought that those will not accept kindly the meddling of another company in their territory."

Jellico grunted. "Kindness and Combine are widely separated in such matters. But we can now take passage on the same ship as your prisoners—"

"But my friend, you have not yet seen the preserve. I assure you that *this* time there shall be no trouble. We have several days yet before you must return to your ship—"

The captain of the *Queen* held up his hand. "Nothing would give me greater pleasure than to inspect the Zoboru preserve, sir—next year. As it is, my holiday is over and the *Queen* is waiting for us on Xecho. Also, permit me to send you some tapes dealing with the newest types of flitters—guaranteed against failures."

"Yes, guaranteed," Tau added guilelessly, "not to break down, lose course, or otherwise disrupt a pleasant excursion."

The Chief Ranger threw back his head and his deep-chested laughter was echoed from the heights above them. "Very well, Captain. Your mail run will bring you back to Xecho at intervals. Meanwhile I shall study your sales tapes concerning the non-expendable flitters. But you *shall* visit Zoboru—and pleasantly, very pleasantly, I assure you, Medic Tau!"

"I wonder," Tau muttered and Dane heard. "Just now the quiet of deep space is a far, far more entrancing propostion!"

ANDRE NORTON
